# The Mirrored World

"With evocative, rich prose and deep emotional resonance, Debra Dean has once again drawn me into a world about which I know little—this time, the imagined history of Xenia of Saint Petersburg. With her new novel, *The Mirrored World*, Dean delivers a compelling and captivating story that touches the soul. Truly a wonderful read."

—Garth Stein, bestselling author of
*The Art of Racing in the Rain*

"*The Mirrored World* explores the mysteries of love, grief, and devotion. Against a vivid backdrop of eighteenth century St. Petersburg and Catherine the Great's royal court, the woman who would become St. Xenia is brought fully to life. Is there a more imaginative, elegant storyteller than Debra Dean?"

—Ann Hood, bestselling author of *The Knitting Circle*

"Love affairs, rivalries, intrigues, prophecy, cross-dressing, madness, sorrow, poverty—*The Mirrored World* is a litany of both the homely and the miraculous. Intimate and richly appointed, Debra Dean's imperial St. Petersburg is as sumptuous and enchanted as the Winter Palace."

—Stewart O'Nan, bestselling author of *Last Night at the Lobster*

"Debra Dean breathes life into the distant figure of Xenia, turning her from a dusty religious icon into a flesh-and-blood woman who channeled the greatest pain of her young life . . . into a mission from God. . . . Dean writes with an internal focus and a wistful grace that suit the subject and the time period. In her skilled hands, history comes alive. . . . Dean takes the bare framework of an extraordinary life and weaves an absorbing and intimate story of devotion around it. Though the world she creates is harsh and cold at times, it is the warmth at its center—the power of love— that stays with you in the end."

—*Miami Herald*

"In her excellent second novel, *The Mirrored World*, Debra Dean has composed a resonant and compelling tale. . . . Dean's writing is superb; she uses imagery natural to the story and an earlier time."

—*Seattle Times*

"For those familiar with the story of St. Xenia, this is a gratifying take on a compelling woman. For others, Dean's vivid prose and deft pacing make for a quick and entertaining read."

—*Publishers Weekly*

"Dean returns to Russia with a concise yet inspiring look at its beloved St. Xenia. . . . Dean's novel grows more profound and affecting with every page."                                —*Booklist*

"Dean made a skyrocketing literary debut with *The Madonnas of Leningrad* and follows up with a meditative spiritual saga that honors its subject with an artful recreation of Xenia's era. Subtle period details and dramatic facts of the eighteenth century enliven this fictional biography."                        —*Library Journal*

"A breathtaking novel of love and madness. . . .Transporting readers to St. Petersburg during the reign of Catherine the Great, Dean brilliantly reconstructs and reimagines the life of St. Xenia, one of Russia's most revered and mysterious holy figures, in a richly told and thought-provoking work of historical fiction."

—Bookreporter.com

# The Mirrored World

ALSO BY DEBRA DEAN

⁓

*Confessions of a Falling Woman*

*The Madonnas of Leningrad*

The

# Mirrored World

## A Novel

# Debra Dean

HARPER ⊙ PERENNIAL

NEW YORK • LONDON • TORONTO • SYDNEY • NEW DELHI • AUCKLAND

HARPER  PERENNIAL

*FIC*
*DEA*

## AUTHOR'S NOTE

This is a work of fiction. While I have tried not to contravene what is known, I have invented between the lines of history. This story should not be read as a factual rendering of the historical personages or events that appear herein.

A hardcover edition of this book was published in 2012 by Harper, an imprint of HarperCollins Publishers.

P.S.™ is a trademark of HarperCollins Publishers.

FIRST HARPER PERENNIAL EDITION PUBLISHED 2013.

*Designed by William Ruoto*

The Library of Congress has catalogued the hardcover edition as follows:

Dean, Debra, 1957– author.
  The mirrored world : a novel / by Debra Dean. — First edition.
    pages cm
  ISBN 978-0-06-123145-2 (Hardcover)
  ISBN 978-0-06-221855-1 (International Edition)
  1.  Courts and courtiers—Fiction. 2.  Russia—History—1689–1801—Fiction. 3.  Saint Petersburg (Russia)—History—18th century—Fiction. I. Title.
  PS3604.E149M57 2012
  813'.6—dc23

                                                          2012015991

ISBN 978-0-06-123146-9 (pbk.)

13 14 15 16 17  OV/RRD  10 9 8 7 6 5 4 3 2 1

FOR MY MOTHER, BEVERLY A. TAYLOR

For if we genuinely love Him . . .
we awaken as the Beloved
in every last part of our body.

—Saint Symeon the Theologian

# CONTENTS

# The Ice Palace

## CHAPTER ONE

Yes, this was her house many years ago, when she was still Xenia. The things you see here—the few furnishings, the books and mementos—they are mine. I have sold and given away much; only a little remains. A feather. This stone with a white ring round it. A bird's skull. Look how delicate it is, thinner than porcelain. This scrap of gold lace from the sleeve of a court dress. I have reached an age when I can see how little all my possessions were worth and even to feel them as a burden on my soul. But the effort to rid myself of it all . . . as Xenia once said, the things of the world cling like vines.

As it happens, this is doubly true of those possessions which are immaterial—the griefs and fears, my reason which I have prized beyond measure, the memories that feel like the sum of me. I am not a holy fool who can give these up.

THE EARLIEST MEMORY—BLACKNESS, AND IN this blackness the sound of church bells clanging wildly—it is of her coming. Clambering down from the bed I share with my *nyanya*, a treacherous descent in the dark, I go to the window. The dusky summer sky is shimmering. Orange, violet, red—the northern lights pulse and flare—and in the street, a man falls to his knees and crosses himself. People are shouting, their words a blur but infused with unmistakable urgency. A riderless white horse careens into view. It rears up and then races on, its tail and mane flying like ragged sails behind it. Frightened, I return to the bed and press my body against Olga's. The next image is that of our bedroom door bursting open and through it, an enormous wolf entering. The wolf says, quite calmly, that its house is afire.

For years, I believed this to be an uncommonly vivid dream. It was only much later, upon hearing my nurse talking about events long past—as old ones are wont to do, as I am doing even now—that I recognized in her story certain unmistakable features of my dream.

There was a terrible fire late in the summer of 1736, the sixth year of Her Imperial Majesty Anna Ioannovna's reign and the fourth year of my life. The fire was said to have begun in a stable near what is now Sadovaya Street, but it spread like a storm through the city. People fled their homes with only those few things they could carry, icons and tableware, a handful of jewelry, whatever they had snatched up in their alarm. One man was seen dragging his bed through the street. An old woman was found in her nightclothes, clutching a squawking goose to her breast. There was no fire brigade then, nor means to draw water from the canals, and in the end over two thousand houses were lost. What I mistook for the northern lights was the entire Admiralty district being consumed by flames.

What I took for a wolf was Xenia. Her mother had escaped their home carrying a daughter in her arms, five rubles in a velvet purse, and a sausage that had been hanging on the larder door. She crossed the pontoon bridge over the Neva, her elder daughter and a servant trailing behind, and walked until she came upon a house she knew, belonging to her husband's cousin. They arrived at our doorstep in the middle of the night. The houseman carried Xenia to my bed, still bundled in a fur lap robe and slung on his shoulder.

"You shrieked at the sight of her," Olga told me later. "I could not calm you."

After the fire, Olga's place in the bed was taken by Xenia and her sister, Nadya. Their father and mine were off fighting the Turks, and so while the city was rebuilding they lived with us. By Olga's account, I slept fitfully for weeks afterwards, plagued by night terrors. What I recall is the sound of howling. Petersburg was much smaller then, muddy and raw and shadowed by forest, and at night one might still hear wolves. I could not help myself, I clutched at Xenia because my nurse was not there. I whimpered to her my fear that the wolves were coming to eat us.

"They are not hungry," she whispered. "They are singing."

I was not so easily mollified. It did not sound like singing.

"That is because you are not a wolf. Listen. She is singing of how lonesome she is." The long wail did indeed sound bereft. After a while, a second voice joined the first. "There, her mate is answering. It must be a very beautiful sound to her."

She twined her arms round me. "I am here, Dashenka. You are not alone." On the word "alone," she made her voice rise into a howl. I giggled.

"Now you answer," she said.

"What?"

"You must sing, too."

I answered her howls with my own until Nadya snapped at us to be still and let her sleep.

It was intended that they stay only until their father returned, but he perished the following year at the storming of Ochakiv. Their future was resettled in that moment. They remained, and I forgot that there had ever been a time before them.

Whatever we know as children, this is the world, eaten whole and without question. So it was with Xenia: I did not think her strange, though an accounting of her features alone would set her apart. She was tall and thin as a willow slip, her nose and chin were rather too sharp, and her pale hair so fine that it continually escaped ribbons and combs. When she moved, wisps lifted and floated about her head, giving her the unkempt and airy appearance of a dandelion blown to seed. Following the science of physiognomy, one might discover her character by this and also by her eyes, which were uncommonly bright but of no definite hue, being very green in one light but the color of hazelnuts in another.

I am reminded of a curiosity we saw as children, housed in the Kunstkamera. This device resembled a sailor's eye-glass. However, peering into the eyepiece, one did not view the ordinary world beyond the glass. Improbably, the horizon filled with brightly colored shards of light, a brilliant mosaic that could be made to break apart and re-form into endless new patterns simply by turning a small knob. It did not seem possible that a narrow brass tube could contain so huge and magnificent a wonder, and yet it did.

Some few days after we visited the museum, I remember, Xenia picked up a feather from the ground and was as giddy as if she had found a ruby in the dirt.

She held it up to the light. "Look."

It is a raven's feather, I thought. My countenance must have shown my ignorance.

"It is black, but look what happens." She rolled the quill slowly between her fingers. "Do you see it, the blue? And now emerald . . ." Colors shimmered on its oily surface. "And there is purple! And even red. It is like the Kaleido-scope!"

I saw then that it was an astonishing feather.

When I parroted her admiration, she handed it to me without a blink. "It is yours," she said. In this same manner, she later gifted me with the bird's skull and the skipping stone and various insects and wildflowers—my own museum of wonders and curiosities.

What consumed her one moment was forgotten in the next, but while in the grip of a passion, she could not be swayed from it, no matter how reckless. She ate wild mush-

rooms without first bringing them home for Olga to inspect. She approached mangy cats and dogs in the street
and would coax into friendly submission even those who
warned her off with low growls or arched backs. None ever
bit her, but the reward for her undiscriminating friendliness
was that she smelled of garlic from Olga continually treat-
ing her for ringworm.

One summer, when we were at my family's country
house, she determined that the view of the river must be
incomparable from the vantage of a particular tree limb
stretching out over the water. She knotted her smock round
her waist and, catching at a low branch, shimmied up the
trunk to a high limb and then to a higher one yet.

"Oh, Dasha," she cried. "It is even finer than I imagined. This must be how angels view the world. I wonder
if I can see our house." She wriggled like a caterpillar out
on the limb until she was perched high over the fast water.

"I am an angel," she proclaimed, and held her arms out
from her sides like wings.

When she fell, the water closed over her and she disappeared. I splashed into the river and stopped shin-deep,
stricken. A little farther downriver she reemerged, gasping
and thrashing at the surface, then sank and did not come
up again.

Like Lot's wife, who turned into a pillar of salt, I was still
gazing on the place where she had last gone down when I
heard her call out.

"Here I am."

Turning, I saw her staggering up the towpath. Her wet

smock was pasted onto her dripping skin, and she alternated between coughing and laughing.

"I am a fallen angel."

A WORLD THAT HAS ANGELS must also have its demons. In the way of children, rank within our little society was determined by our relative ages. By virtue of a year, Xenia's sister, Nadya, might order us about and strike us without cause, and she was not shy to do either.

One of our pastimes was to reenact stories we had heard from our mothers. Nadya played a grand duchess or a German princess, Xenia was the noble lady's younger sister or a lady-in-waiting, and I was cast as a servant. My little brother, Vanya, served as was needed for a pet spaniel or monkey. In whatever configuration, though, the game turned on Nadya's being endlessly demanding and capricious. She might send one of us to fetch something, a ribbon for her hair or a tray of sweetmeats, but when we returned with the imaginary item, invariably the ribbon was the wrong color—she wanted the green, not the yellow—the sweets were inferior, and she had not asked for her pet monkey after all but for her parrot.

Once, she asked me to bring a letter that had recently been sent her by an admirer. Dutifully, I left our room, waited a bit, and then returned with the imaginary missive.

"Well, where is it?" Nadya demanded.

"Here, my lady," I said, and pretended to pinch something between my thumb and forefinger.

"No, fool. The letter I want is in the drawer of my dressing table. It is tied with a blue ribbon."

I broke the spell of the game. "Do you mean my father's letter?" I whispered, like an actor seeking a prompt.

She glared at me with convincing menace. "*My* letter. Bring it here this instant, before I lose patience."

I remained motionless, considering whether to go out into the passage and try again.

She rebuked me with a slap. "Go!" she shrieked.

I ran to my mother's dressing room and slid open the drawer. Inside was a fine handkerchief of embroidered linen that had been given to her by Grand Duchess Anna Petrovna when my mother left her service to be married. Next to this was the packet of letters written by my father. The most recent had arrived only the previous day. My mother had sent for the priest to read it to her and take down a reply, and afterwards had put it away here, together with the others.

I hesitated. On occasion, I had been allowed to open the drawer and look at the handkerchief, but never to disturb the contents. If I were discovered, I would be punished, but if I did not return to Nadya with the letter I should also be punished. Weighing the two dangers, I chose to dodge that which was nearer. I slipped the thin envelope from the top of the packet and carried it back to Nadya.

"Here, my lady."

She took it from me and opened the envelope. Glancing cursorily over the paper, Nadya read aloud: " 'To the most beautiful lady in all of Russia—' "

"Is that what it says?" I asked.

"Of course."

"But I mean, truly?"

"Are you calling me a liar?"

I did not know how Nadya might have learnt to read. Still, it was the accepted condition of being youngest that everyone was gifted with knowledge unavailable to me.

" 'To the most beautiful lady in all of Russia,' " she began again. The letter went on to proclaim my father's admiration in many florid phrases. He pleaded that my mother send some sign that his affection was reciprocated.

I had no memory of my father, though he had been a constant, unseen presence in our household. His name was repeated in our daily prayers, and when any decision was to be made, my mother invoked him, wondering aloud if Nikolai Feodosievich would approve of this or that.

" 'If you do not care for me,' " Nadya continued to read, " 'I shall surely die.' "

I was caught in the spell of hearing his words and peered over her shoulder that I might see them as well. "What is this?" I asked, pointing to an intriguing shape like a rowboat reflected on water.

"That? That means 'send.' "

"And this?"

"That is 'die.' It's simple," Nadya said. "Look." She drew her finger slowly under a line of mysterious strokes and curls and pronounced their meaning. " 'To the most beautiful princess in all of the Russias.' Now you read it."

I tried to link the images to words, but what had meant "send" in one line meant something else in the next.

"I cannot."

"It is the same words," Nadya snapped. "'To the most beautiful princess . . .' Just repeat what I say."

But I wanted to read it for myself. I stared fixedly at the place where Nadya pointed and saw what looked like snippets of black hair. Flour laced with weevils. A regiment of tiny soldiers on new snow. But no meaning in any of it. The insects on the page blurred.

"Look!" Nadya pointed to an inky puddle on the paper. "Now you have spoilt it."

I began to cry in earnest.

"Be quiet," Nadya snarled. "They will hear you." Her warning served only to raise the pitch of my wailing. She pulled off one of her shoes and raised it threateningly. "I said be quiet. Do you want a whipping?"

Xenia also tried to quiet me. "Don't take it to heart, Dashenka. It was only pretend. Nadya can't read either."

When Nadya turned and struck her across the cheek, Xenia did not cry out or even flinch. Oddly, her silence enraged Nadya all the more, who struck her again and then again with more force as though to jar loose some response.

I closed my eyes but could not shut out the sound, over and over, of leather on flesh. Then it slowed and stopped.

When I peeked through my fingers, they stood just as they had, Nadya with the shoe raised above her head, and Xenia facing her, but Xenia . . . How may I tell this? Though her flesh was pocked with welts, she looked as though she had eaten something airy and sweet and was still holding the taste on her tongue.

Nadya's hand began to tremble, and she could not meet Xenia's bright gaze without glancing away again. As though Xenia were willing it, she slowly lowered her arm.

I COULD NOT SEE IT then, any more than one can see the pattern on the back side of a tapestry. A knight, a swan, a ring of flowers—on the reverse they are only a muddle of color, the woof and warp of tangled threads picked up and then dropped again.

We passed them in the streets, poor senseless wretches talking to the air. These were women without husbands or children, without any history to lend them meaning. So far as we knew, they had always been there. One amongst these, whom Olga called the Blessed One, lived on the steps of the church. She was always in this same place, wrapped in a filthy sheepskin. Olga would bring her a dish of kasha or a sardine and set it at her feet, but the old woman never thanked her or acknowledged by a look that she knew us. She stared straight before her like a horse asleep on its feet, or she ranted to unseen presences whom she accused of terrible crimes. Olga said we must show her pity, but she was terrifying, bedraggled and toothless, and it was like trying to find pity for a toad or a wolf.

As we were coming out of the church one morning, the old woman suddenly reached out and caught hold of Xenia. Pinned, Xenia thrashed and tried to escape her grip, but the old one held fast and, by looking into Xenia's eyes, seemed to enchant her into stillness.

"This one sees," the old woman pronounced.

Olga crossed herself. "What? What does she see, Blessed One?"

The old woman released Xenia's wrist. "Ask her yourself."

But Xenia was wide-eyed with terror. She stared back at the Blessed One and would not answer.

At the time, I assumed she was afraid of the old woman. Now I wonder if she was not more afraid of what the old woman saw in her.

## CHAPTER TWO

I t may be that I am among the last persons alive to have seen with my own eyes the palace of Empress Anna Ioannovna's jester. Even so, everyone knows the story, and in the telling and retelling, from nurse to child, it has acquired the patina of a fairy tale. I have sometimes seen my son, Matvey, smile indulgently when I have said to other guests that I was there and all this is true. I do not fault him. Even to me, the memory seems implausible, but this is just as it happened.

When she was young, the future empress was betrothed to a German duke. Her uncle, the great Tsar Peter, had arranged the marriage and had brought the duke to Russia for a spectacular wedding. There were many weeks of raucous celebration, and on the last night before the new couple were to leave for his homeland, the Tsar challenged the young groom to a drinking contest. Tsar Peter was a man of great appetites, and had the duke known his reputation perhaps he would have declined the challenge. Then again, dukes are not made to be humble. He drank himself into a stupor and fell ill, and on the journey back to Courland with his new wife he died. Though Anna Ioannovna implored her uncle that she be allowed to return to Petersburg, the Tsar wished it otherwise, and so she lived friendless in a foreign country for twenty years until Peter died and she was allowed to return home as Empress of all the Russias.

Because she was cruelly widowed and then prevented by the burdens of state from marrying the man she loved, it became a favorite sport of the Empress's to arrange the marriages of those beneath her. And thus it was that she contrived to celebrate her birthday and the end of the war with the Turks by marrying her jester to one of her maids.

The nuptials were held at Shrovetide, in the midst of the most brutal winter in memory. People and cattle alike froze on the sides of roads. Birds dropped like stones from out of the sky. Nearly as strange for me, my father returned that winter from the war. I was eight years of age.

It was a shock to have him appear in the flesh. Alongside God, he had been the invisible center of our lives, and in my childish mind my earthly and heavenly fathers had blurred together as one. He looked very much as I imagined God might, tall, with a gray head and barrel chest, very stern and imposing. Even more fearsome, the outer part of his left ear was missing.

He greeted my mother restrainedly, and when she presented him with the son she had borne in his absence, he felt Vanya's calves and arms, as one might inspect a new horse, and nodded his approval. "He is sturdy."

My mother drew me forward from behind her skirts. "This is Dasha." He eyed me solemnly. I was certain he could hear the loud tolling of my heart, and I braced myself to be inspected also, but apparently this was not needed.

"And these are Grigoriy Ivanovich's daughters, Nadya and Xenia."

Xenia flew to him, her arms thrown out, and called him Uncle Kolya. Whether surprised or not, pleased or not, the set of his features hardly shifted, but after a moment's hesitation he obliged her with a kiss and a pat on the head. After this, Nadya also presented her cheek to be kissed. He then turned back to me, expectant. Taking my shoulders in his huge hands, he bent down from his great height. The gash of his ear loomed red and ragged in my vision, and the stubble of his beard raked across my cheek. I burst into tears.

"What is this?" he said.

"She is afraid of everything," Nadya told him.

I have never forgotten his eye clouding over like a pond with a thin skin of ice. He may have misconstrued my shyness as a want of feeling, but it was not so. I haunted the doorway outside whatever room he was in, held rapt by his voice—a rumble that seemed to begin in the cellar—but if his notice should happen to fall on me, I froze.

Of course, Xenia was not afraid of him. On the contrary, she was rash in her affections and whenever he came home would throw herself at his person with cries of "Uncle Kolya! Uncle Kolya!" Though he was not unkind, I think he was unsure how to answer such insistent affection from one who was, after all, only another dependent. It was Nadya, caring the least, who made herself easiest for him to love. She brought him his slippers and pipe and he rewarded her by absently patting her head and calling her his little lieutenant before turning his attention elsewhere.

With his homecoming, a festive disorder unraveled the quiet habits we had formerly observed. My mother and Aunt Galya, excited to return to society, left us children almost entirely to the care of servants. Meals were arranged round the drills of my father's regiment, and in the evenings there were suppers and dances that kept them away till morning. Sometimes, though, we were allowed into their rooms as they dressed. We helped to tie their hoops and lace their stays, and we listened to them gossip about who had worn what or danced with whom on the previous night.

For weeks beforehand, much of their talk concerned preparations for the jester's wedding. As best I could piece together, the jester had formerly been one of the Empress's advisors but had done something to provoke her displeasure and had been sentenced to death for this. But rather than have him executed, the Empress in her mercy stripped him of his title and made him her jester and cupbearer. Now she was going to marry him off to one of her servants. It was to be a great spectacle. Hundreds of exotic peoples were being brought in from the farthest reaches of the empire to lead the wedding procession. And hidden from view by high wooden barriers, something was being erected on the frozen river for the nuptials.

On the morning of the wedding, Olga took us to watch my father in the parade. A throng, festive in spite of the bitter cold, lined Neva Prospect. From far up the avenue, we could hear cheers and the percussion of military music, and then we saw the approach of the regiments. Mounted officers were flanked six-deep, their red breeches and green coats repeated over and over like the infinite reflections between two mirrors. As the Semeonovsky regiment passed, we scanned the rows of officers until we spotted my father, a full head taller than his fellows and looking grand as a statue on his bay horse. As he passed, we cheered loudly. Though he did not break his somber gaze, I felt sure he saw us. We followed him down the avenue, threading through the crowd and keeping pace with his progress until we reached the Admiralty Meadow, where the regiments broke off like ice floes into an open sea of horses and uniformed soldiers. We lost sight of him momentarily, but then Xenia spied him again. He was in the company of a fellow officer who often brought sweets to the house and whom we called Uncle Petya.

"Uncle Kolya! Uncle Petya!" she cried.

Astride their horses, they moved in our direction, soldiers and onlookers parting like the Red Sea at their approach. They brought their mounts alongside us. My father said to Olga, "I thought I saw my daughter in the street, but I told myself I must be mistaken." I could not read in his aspect whether he approved or not.

"They wished to see you ride in the parade."

"No, I think they have come to see the elephant," Uncle

Petya said. "Is that not so, girls?" He looked up the avenue. "Ah, even as I speak . . ."

What looked to be a mud-and-wattle hut was erected in the center of the avenue on four stone gray pillars. Atop this was strapped an iron cage, like a second storey. The whole contraption towered over the onlookers, of a scale more rightly associated with the surrounding buildings than with a living creature. But the pillars were not stationary after all, and they were bearing the hut towards us.

Even when I recognized it as an animal, its features were bewildering. What appeared to be a long tail hung from the approaching end, swaying from side to side like a pendulum. Flaps like dusty carpets waved at each side of its head. It had no fur but was cloaked in an ill-fitting gray hide that hung from its bones like poorly tanned leather, and in its lumbering wake it left a trail of prints in the snow as large and deep as soup tureens. As it drew alongside us, the beast's eye looked out at the world with the patience of an elderly monk.

Within the cage on the elephant's back was the bridal couple. In their appearance they were as startling as the beast on which they were conveyed. The woman was dressed in the finery of a bride, but her face was shriveled as an old cabbage, and she shrugged beneath the weight of a large hump growing from her left shoulder. The groom, decades younger than she, was the most unhappy man I had ever seen. Something in his glum physiognomy was familiar.

The crowd began to hoot and make clucking noises.

"It's the Easter hen!" Xenia said.

"What's this?" Uncle Petya asked.

Xenia told him where we had last seen the bridegroom: on the previous Easter, he had been made to sit in a huge straw nest at the entrance to the Winter Palace and give out eggs as gifts from the Empress. When commanded, he would begin to cluck, to bob his chin and flap his arms, and then he would withdraw from beneath himself a colored egg for the petitioner. What had made the performance amusing to the crowd was his great, pained dignity: even as he flapped his arms like wings, his expression had remained that of a man trying by force of will to rise above his own ridiculousness.

"I do not think he liked to give up his eggs," Xenia said.

Uncle Petya laughed. "I should not want to give up my eggs, either. What say you to that, Nikolai Feodosievich? Would you not be sad to give up your eggs?"

My father remained grave. "I say that Prince Golitsyn should have considered this before he defied his sovereign to marry."

"Is that why he looks so sad?" Xenia asked.

"This wife is his punishment for the first. She was a papist."

Xenia asked my father what was a papist, and he answered that it was one who followed the Pope in Rome.

"Is it wrong to marry a papist?"

"It is a sin. And an even weightier sin to defy the Empress to do it."

Her eyes followed the iron cage. "Did he love the papist very, very much?"

My father's expression hardened slightly more. "That does not matter. It is too dear a price."

"I shall pay more, I think."

Behind the bride and groom, scores of couples were parading two by two astride all manner of beasts. It was akin to Noah's menagerie, had he been asked to collect two of each people as well. A couple with the tawny skin and slant eyes of Tatars rode on camels. A pair of Finns followed on dogs, others on bulls, donkeys, miniature horses, and reindeer. The riders themselves were as various as the beasts that bore them, and were costumed in curious native garb. A Tatar bride with a ring in her nose balanced atop her head a tall red beehive ornamented with pieces of tin and coins. Her dress was similarly adorned with bells, so that she jangled musically as she rode. A red-haired pair from the far North was clothed from hood to boot in fancifully worked skins, and another couple, the man indistinguishable from his mate, was costumed in pantaloons with an open skirt and sash.

"Now, there's a striking fellow," Uncle Petya said. The man he indicated resembled the knights in old tales, clad in a tight-fitting waistcoat and breeches and carrying a bow and quiver. He had long whiskers, and his head was capped with metal like a silvered melon. "Xenia, would you like your uncle to buy you a husband like that? He is not your Prince Golitsyn, but I'll wager he's a prince of some sort."

Xenia was strangely quiet and only shook her head.

"No? What of you, Dasha? What, no takers for this fine fellow?" Uncle Petya turned to Nadya. "But I am forgetting myself; it is the eldest sister who chooses first."

"Doesn't he already have a wife?" Nadya asked.

"Quite right," Uncle Petya said with mock solemnity. "He does. Ah well, girls, don't despair. There are a hundred more here to choose from. We shall find you husbands yet."

There was not quite a hundred more but so many that by the time the last couple brought up the rear of the pageant they were trailed by lamplighters, and the Admiralty clock was chiming three.

I did not understand then what I know now, that half the jest lay in asking us our opinion. Tsar Peter had made it law that a girl could not be married without her consent, but it was a law observed mostly in the breach. No good father would allow such an important decision as marriage to rest on the affectionate inclinations or disinclinations of a girl. To be led by the heart was foolhardy: one need only look to the terrible fate of Prince Golitsyn to know this.

THE NEXT DAY, WE WENT to the river to see the folly that had been built there. All these years later, I cannot recall my first glimpse of it without a shiver. Seen from a distance, the jester's palace seemed to shimmer and float just above the surface of the frozen Neva, a trick of the eye, like a dwarfed reflection of the Imperial palace looming on the far shore. As we approached, though, the chimera did not dissolve. If anything, it grew more wondrous.

In every aspect but size it was the counterfeit of a real palace—it had fine windows and even a pediment adorned with statues—but it was fashioned entirely from ice. Guarding it were cannons also made of ice, and at intervals they fired crystalline balls. Two glassy rows of statuary shaped like potted orange trees beckoned us towards the front doors. We walked past the balustrades. Through milky blue walls, shadowy figures could be seen moving about within. It had the appearance of a spectral dwelling that housed souls caught between this life and the next. Night hovered close at the gloomy edges of the February afternoon. Another cannon report shattered the air like thunder.

We climbed the steps. Passing through a doorframe resembling translucent green marble, we entered into the cold blue light of the anteroom. The room and everything in it was fashioned from ice. Light glowed softly through the walls. Objects shimmered like apparitions and rather than casting shadows emitted a subtle radiance. The effect of this was to confuse the senses. As one moved, shapes emerged from the air, what was not quite visible from one perspective taking form when viewed from another angle. On the longer wall of the room, artisans had etched the counterfeit of a tapestry showing a stag-hunting scene. The finely detailed picture could only be viewed straight on; I stepped to one side and the stag and its pursuers vanished. As I moved back again, they reappeared. How long I was thus occupied I do not know, but when I looked up, Xenia and Olga and Nadya had all disappeared. A doorway wavered at the far end of the room, and through it I saw shadows walking about in the blue gloom, but a tingling unease kept me from passing through the door. Instead, I waited. A cluster of people was gathered before a table, and I inserted myself amongst them. On the table stood a clock;

it was this they were admiring. One could see through the face of the clock and into a glassy interior filled with an intricate mechanism of cogs and gears.

"It doesn't move." Nadya was suddenly beside me.

"What?" I asked.

"It's made of ice, you goose. It will say eight o'clock for as long as you stand here."

"I thought it might chime."

I was foolish, she said. Telling me that she and Xenia had found something much better, she pulled me into the hall beyond the anteroom.

A table had been laid there. Glimmering plates and wineglasses and cutlery that seemed made of fine crystal awaited the pleasure of diners. Ice tapers stood in ice candelabra, ready to be lit, and serving platters held a glittering cluster of grapes, a transparent loaf of bread, a wedge that looked like cheese. As with the clock, every article resembled its counterpart in the world but was drained of color and substance, like a soul removed from its body. All except for this: on a small table in the corner of the room, three playing cards were frozen into the surface. They were just ordinary cards—a two of hearts, a knave, an eight of clubs—but amidst all the translucent delicacies of the room they appeared shockingly solid and coarse.

I ran my fingers over them, fascinated. "Look. They are real."

Nadya shrugged. "What of it? They must have played cards last night."

"Who?" I asked.

"That is what I have been trying to show you! The jester and his bride spent their wedding night here." She was passing through the far doorway. I followed.

Here was a dressing table ornamented with various combs and brushes, pots and perfume bottles, and over the dressing table was a large, ornate mirror. The mirror was so perfect a counterfeit that I thoughtlessly glanced into it. I went sick with fright: there was no reflection. My limbs felt weightless, and as I looked into the gleaming blankness the disquieting thought rose up in me that I, too, had become a spirit.

"Come here," Nadya said. At the center of the chamber, an enormous canopied bed had been chiseled, and draperies spilt to the floor round it like frozen waterfalls. Nadya stood beside it, and Xenia was there also, staring into the interior. Though apprehensive, I approached as though unseen forces were pushing me from behind.

"Look," Nadya commanded, and then her voice dropped to a whisper. "This morning, the guards found them here. They were frozen dead in each other's arms."

Trembling, I made myself peer beyond the curtains. I expected to find Prince Golitsyn and his hunchbacked bride, their limbs locked in a stiff embrace, their flesh and bones translated to ice. But to my vast relief, there was nothing, nothing but sculpted pillows and bedclothes.

"You can see where they lay," Nadya said. It was true: at the center of the bed, the ice had melted slightly and left a shallow depression. It was not hard to imagine the shape of two persons lying side by side.

A strangled whimper came from Xenia. I followed her stricken gaze and looked again into the bed. Frozen into the surface of a pillow was a ragged tuft of hair. It was bloody at the roots where shreds of scalp still adhered.

IT HAS BEEN SAID THAT they were brought straight from the church, and that Empress Anna's guests complained at being made to step out of their carriages and follow the bridal couple out onto the river, where an icy wind cut through their wraps. But their sniping was silenced by the sight of the palace glittering in the frigid moonlight. Inside, they admired the cunning forgeries and paid lavish compliments to the Empress and the architect Eropkin on such a magnificent conception.

Golitsyn and the hunchbacked old maid were whisked into the bedchamber. There, the two were made to undress and were left naked. Guards were set at the door. It being customary on a wedding night to feast while the bride and groom consummate their union, the Empress Anna and her guests then hurried on to the banquet, their receding torches making a trail across the ice.

The particulars of what was said and done between Prince Golitsyn and the old maid after they were left alone in the darkness of their monstrous tomb—these things can no more be discovered than can the secrets of any other wedding night.

What is known is that they were found the next morning in the posture of husband and wife, lying in each other's arms. And although their deaths were widely reported, they had survived the night—if only just—by virtue of the hunchback's cleverness. While undressing, she had hid a pearl in her cheek, and this she later traded to one of the guards for his sheepskin coat. Bride and groom shared the warmth of the other's body wrapped in this.

Though the old woman was dead of a cold within the week, years later Xenia would find a happy ending in the story. The wretched hunchback, lonely and unloved all her days, had saved the life of her husband and died a married woman. "I should have prayed for a fate so kind," she confided.

# Learning to Mate

## CHAPTER THREE

In 1745, my thirteenth year, there were three more weddings, but so far as the populace of Petersburg was concerned, only one worthy of mention.

A German princess had been brought to the court the previous year for the purpose of providing Empress Elizabeth's nephew with a wife. The general opinion was that she was hardly a beauty, but her ingratiating manner and the earnestness with which she applied herself to learning Russian had won her allies. It was hoped she might provide some needed ballast for the queer young man whom Fate had put in line for the throne.

The marriage of Catherine to Grand Duke Peter was to be the first royal wedding ever celebrated in Petersburg, and the Empress was determined it should rival in splendor the recent wedding of the Dauphin at Versailles. To this end, the whole town was cast into a frenzy of preparation. Sergei Naryshkin, it was rumored, had spent seven thousand rubles to refurbish his carriage and inlay its wheels with mirror. Tailors were already at work designing new livery for Leonid Vladimirovich Berevsky's pages and footmen. Throughout the capital, nobles vied with one another to secure the last good bottles of wine and the services of the best musicians and chefs, and for any of these things the usual currencies of bribery and flattery were much increased.

This spirit of extravagance entered our household as well. Having turned seventeen, Nadya was to be brought out into society that season, and in anticipation of this Aunt Galya had purchased pandoras, little dolls imported from Paris and dressed *à la mode* so that a dressmaker might copy the fashions. Bolts of fabric were brought to the house for our mothers' perusal, together with a quantity of ribbons and laces. It was decided between them that one court dress would not be adequate, and then there were further expenses to be incurred for morning dresses, shoes, and fans, and for bribes to arrange invitations.

"Perhaps this is not needed after all?" Aunt Galya handed a card of lace to my mother so that she might be contradicted.

"You might leave the neck plain," my mother said, "but the dress will not look finished without a bit of lace at the sleeves." She grew thoughtful. "It's a pity Dasha is too young to be brought out this year. She might profit by some other occupation for her mind."

"You mustn't fret about Dashenka," Aunt Galya said. "She will make some man a good wife."

"Only if she can first be cured of her bad habits."

The habits to which my mother referred were in truth only one, but it was sufficient to be more worrisome to her than many smaller ones. On several occasions, I had been found staring at the pages of the Psalter. At first this had been mistaken for piety and no thought had been given to it, but then I had made the error of confessing to Olga that I was trying to read.

"No, no, kitten." Olga corrected me gently, and, closing the book, returned it to its place. "You do not want to do that. It makes a woman barren."

There was no fate so fearful as this, and Olga's warning should have been sufficient to cure me of my fault, but it was not. I had such a hunger for words that I took to spying on my brother whilst he was at his lessons. Afterwards, I would hide myself in the wardrobe for hours, the Psalter opened on my lap and a candlestick set on the floor beside me. In its flickering light, the strokes and curls on the pages slowly began to yield their mysteries. Then Nadya had found me and reported to my mother. I was whipped not only for my disobedience but also for taking a taper into the wardrobe and thereby endangering the lives of my family.

Now, fingering the lace, my mother lamented, "What man will want a girl who defies her parents to read?"

"I've heard that the German princess is fond of books," Aunt Galya said, but this was no comfort to my mother.

"My daughter can ill afford such quirks."

Aunt Galya hit upon an inspiration. "Why not bring her out with Nadya? She is young, as you say, but such a season will not come again with all its chances to make a match. And if it happens not this year, she will have that many more years to try."

My aunt pleased herself further with the argument that in truth it would represent an economy to bring out all three girls at once. We might share dresses and ribbons and whatnot, and the savings from this could even be put towards engaging a French dance master.

ON THE MORNING OF OUR first dancing lesson, Olga dressed us in our mothers' hoops and skirts. We were further outfitted with heeled slippers, fans, and little porcelain bonbonnieres. So attired, we seemed suddenly to outgrow our childhood and the confines of our bedroom as well. With whalebone panniers strapped to our hips, our skirts extended us each to the width of three persons, and we maneuvered in the small room like the square-rigged ships one sees crowding the Neva, under full sail and narrowly avoiding collision at every tack. Only by turning sideways were we able to pass through the door and sidle down the corridor to the drawing room. Though my mother's slippers were stuffed to hold my foot, and the extra length of her skirt pinned up so that I should not trip, I preened, newly a lady, and anticipated the impression I would make on the dance master.

When finally he was announced, though, it was he who was to be admired, not we. Monsieur La Roche was a knob-kneed man with rotting teeth and a horsehair wig so puny that it rested atop his own hair like a weasel slaughtered and powdered to serve the purpose. But as befitted one who was French, he was full of condescension. As we were introduced, only the languid transfer of his gaze from one of us to the next distinguished him from a portrait. Without breaking his pose, he uttered a few syllables in his native tongue. As Monsieur La Roche spoke no Russian, our instruction was conducted entirely in French, a language known to us formerly only through our mothers speaking the occasional phrase.

Society may be a masquerade, but I discovered that it was not sufficient merely to don the costume. As with any theatrical, there were lines to be learnt and attitudes to be committed to memory, and with them the intricate language of the fan by which such attitudes were signaled. To touch your left cheek with a closed fan meant *no*, the right cheek meant *yes*, and if you then unfurled the fan before your face, this signaled to the observer that you wished him to follow you. A dozen different meanings were assigned to fluttering the fan, depending upon rapidity and placement.

It was too much for me to remember, hampered as I was by my great fear of forgetting. Even a curtsy was more exacting than it appeared. I dipped, positioning my foot precisely so and sweeping my arm out slowly, now sliding my fan open and holding it just so, then casting my eyes downwards in a show of modesty. Resting, I then prepared for the final challenge: to undo all I had just done and haul up the anchor of my skirts whilst conveying the impression of floating.

With painstaking slowness, we progressed to the various figures of the minuet, which were a trial to Xenia as well. She had a natural expansiveness of gesture common to tall people and a restlessness particular to her. Though she might tamp down her spirit to fit the small, slow movements that Monsieur dictated, her face reflected like a glass all the effort it cost her, and she instantly undid any success with a burst of jubilation that caused him to chide her again.

Nadya's talent for imitation answered Monsieur's haughtiness with her own. She even improved upon it. *"Oui, c'est ça exactement!"* he exclaimed as she rose from her curtsy. That she did not care if he praised her seemed to please him all the more—she had mastered the aloofness that underpinned every other attitude. From a resting posture of aloofness, one need make only minute adjustments to signal displeasure or its hardly perceptible opposites, approval or amusement.

After several weeks, Monsieur at last satisfied himself. He posed us each with an imagined partner, and taking himself to the rented pianoforte began to plink its keys. This was Xenia's downfall. She was entranced by the melody: her arms lifted of their own accord, and her head swayed like a daisy in the breezes of the music. Springing off her toes, she gave the impression she might well take flight with the next step.

*"Non, non!"* Monsieur railed at her to be still, but it did him no good. She was sweeping across the floor, lost to delight.

Exasperated, he sent for baskets, and commanded that they be filled with grain and tied to the tops of our heads like hats. This was to encourage a still bearing. Thus burdened, I felt like one of the little horses one sometimes sees in the country half-buried under sheaves of rye. On my little heeled hooves, any movement threatened to topple the load.

He began to play again. Formerly, I had managed to follow most of Monsieur's instructions by observing Nadya. Now I could not do even this for fear that in turning my head, I might spill the grain. Paralyzed by apprehension, I lost the power of locomotion. Monsieur barked out my name and, snapping a finger, issued a command. I could only gape. He left the pianoforte and marched towards me, repeating the command in a Gallic crescendo. I tapped my right cheek with my fan—*yes?*—and then splayed it open rather prettily in the desperate hope this might assuage him. It did not.

"*Non, non, non! Le pied gauche!*" he raged, this time stamping his buckled shoe and gesturing to it.

I stamped my foot in imitation, and a few grains spilt from my basket to the floor. Forgetting, I looked down, and a shower clattered round me like hail.

"*Petite idiote! Pas comme un cheval de fiacre! Avec la délicatesse!*"

"No, stop it!" Xenia commanded. "Do not berate her!"

Monsieur La Roche swiveled on his heel, and I thought he might strike her with his stick, but Xenia stood her ground. Chin lifted, she had the regal bearing of an Empress, never mind that no Empress has ever worn so ridiculous a hat.

"Speak to her in Russian. We will not tell."

His haughty air deflated, and his glance went to Nadya and then round the room to Olga and my brother, Vanya, who sat at the window, and to me again. He looked like a thief who has been caught with his pockets full of his master's silver.

"With the left foot," he muttered. His pronunciation exposed him at once as a Russian. "Delicately. As though you are stepping on live coals."

TWICE A WEEK, EMPRESS ELIZABETH hosted a lavish ball in the Winter Palace. The smaller one was held for some two hundred of Her Imperial Majesty's friends and the inner circle of the court, but several times this number might be invited to the larger of the balls, virtually every person of noble rank in the city minus only those who had earned her displeasure. This was to be our proving ground.

As our mothers maneuvered us through the throng, Xenia scanned the room hungrily. "Dasha"—she elbowed me and jutted her chin upwards—"the Kaleidoscope." Over our heads hung a gilt chandelier, its crystal pendants refracting each flame into a galaxy of lights.

We arrived at a clutch of women on the perimeter, the wives and widows of the Semeonovsky regiment, and our mothers set at once to work, offering commiseration on a husband's gout, congratulations on a son's promotion, and so forth. One might have thought they intended no purpose here except to reassure themselves on the health and well-being of each one of the women's relations. In truth, their goal was this: that one of these women might send a page to retrieve an unattached son or nephew.

"And your youngest," Aunt Galya inquired, "Grigory

Vasilievich, he must be almost grown by now. That is he?"
She feigned shock. "In the blue waistcoat? No, it cannot
be. But he is a man already! The day is long but a lifetime
is short, is it not so? Only yesterday my little Nadya and
Xenia were in their smocks, and look at them now."

Whilst our mothers labored on our behalf, what was required of us was only that we display a quiet demeanor and
be at the ready if called upon. But Xenia could not attend
to this little task. Her concentration continually reeled out
to follow pairs of dancers revolving past us.

"Oh, look!" she cried out. She pointed to a lady's enormous fan of peacock feathers blooming, eye by eye, with
exquisite slowness.

The wives and widows turned as one, first to the spectacle of Xenia's pointing finger and then to the lady with the
peacock fan. Two eyes had been cut out from the feathers,
and through these the lady's own eyes were visible.

The women took note of the fan without wonder.

"It is a poor copy. Princess Dashkova's had the edges
tipped with gold."

It is a commonplace that few who admire a painting have
any acquaintance with a brush. Likewise, those viewing fireworks marvel at the counterfeit of a flaming bird or a flower
blooming in the night sky without a notion how the effect is achieved. But here, the spectators were also the actors.
There was no ruse of the tailor with which they themselves
were unacquainted, no paint they would mistake for a blush.
They, too, had bathed themselves in pigeon water and applied to their own skins pomades and powders and patches.

They, too, had endured hours at the hands of their hairdressers and slept in chairs to preserve the sticky confection atop their heads. As such, they were severe critics of their fellows. Xenia's delight showed a lack of discernment, and it made her seem impressionable as a peasant in their eyes.

When a chorister sang for the assemblage, she gaped at him openly in childish wonder. With his last note, she sprang to her feet and began to applaud with such enthusiasm that she drew the amused notice of those within earshot and then the entire room. She alone was on her feet, still clapping. The chorister gave a little bow in our direction, and this only encouraged her further. I blushed for her who had not the sense to blush for herself. Nadya, more quick-thinking, reached up and pinched Xenia hard.

She yelped.

Nadya hissed behind her fan. "Sit. Down."

If Xenia had forfeited the women's approbation, Nadya redeemed our mothers' efforts by behaving precisely as she had been coached. She said little and not a word of it original or sincere, but the airs that she had practiced in our childhood games and perfected under the tutelage of Monsieur La Roche lent her the slightly bored appearance of one far above her rank. She was invited to dance, and when she did the honors and presented herself before the Empress, it was with the ease of one who had at last found her rightful place. As I watched her turn into the figures of the dance, I adjusted my bodice and scratched hungrily. My corset had long since transformed itself into a torture of binding and itches, but Nadya inhabited her own with the seeming disregard of one who had been swaddled in whalebone.

So fine an impression did Nadya make that she was summoned afterwards to be introduced to Countess Chernysheva. By this notice, her value increased again and even spilt over to Xenia and myself. Partners were produced for us as well. It had been decided beforehand that if I were asked to dance I should make a better impression by declining, but Xenia was allowed to be escorted onto the dance floor at the start of a minuet.

She drew notice round the room, the girl who had applauded the singer. However, I do not think she was aware of it. As she danced, her glance followed the chorister. When her escort whispered something to her shoulder, she startled and looked at him as though trying to place where they had met. At this critical moment, she failed to turn to the left and followed her escort to the right instead. Beside me, Aunt Galya gasped.

The circle of dancers had split into two lines, with Xenia amongst the gentlemen and facing her own sex. Looking up the line, she did some swift mental calculation and then made an ungainly dash across the open field. She wedged herself into the middle of the opposite line and, by so doing, further upset the pattern.

Each dancer was now aligned with a different partner. After the shuffle, Nadya drew an unlucky hand and found herself paired with a rotund courtier old enough to be her grandfather. Stone-eyed, she turned to watch Xenia, happy and oblivious, step out to meet her new partner.

It was this same chorister. He looked at Xenia with the winking amusement he had shown her earlier and made some remark. Her answer caused him to laugh aloud. They stepped forward, and for the remainder of the dance never ceased their bantering. Xenia gazed at him as though he were not a man but some magical being. She forgot her feet, forgot her counting, and as the chorister tipsily wheeled her about the room, they banked like billiard balls off the other dancers. The minuet was too slow to contain them.

At the end of the dance, he delivered Xenia back to us.

"I believe you have lost a daughter?" The chorister bowed low to Aunt Galya with a gallant if unsteady flourish. Recovering his balance, he introduced himself as Colonel Andrei Feodorovich Petrov.

"In truth, I had half a mind to keep her," he confided, "but I would not want it said I am a thief. I have little but my honesty to recommend me to a mother, but perhaps this may earn me the gift of the daughter's company again."

It was a pretty speech, and Aunt Galya and my mother shared the view that there was not such a thing as an innocent remark. They turned their efforts to learning if any merits more than honesty might belong to this Colonel Petrov.

He was from Little Russia and the orphan of a landless noble—not, speaking generally, the lineage of a desirable suitor—but by virtue of his sweet voice Andrei Feodorovich Petrov had been brought as a youth to the Ukrainian chapel choir and there had befriended a fellow chorister.

As my mother was fond of saying, "Tell me who is your

friend and I'll tell you who you are." Colonel Petrov's friend was Count Alexi Razumovsky, whom wags called the "Night Emperor."

Years earlier, when Elizabeth had plucked up the young Razumovsky and made him her favorite, Andrei Feodorovich Petrov had been well placed to catch some of the extravagant droppings that fell from Her Highness's plate. He received from the Grand Duchess a position in the court choir and, after she assumed the throne, a military rank along with a doubling of his salary.

Not that Petrov lacked merits independent of the Empress and the Count. He was pleasantly featured and had the easy manner of one who desires nothing from his friends but their mirth, and so he had many of these. In fact, he seemed to be so universally well-liked that not even the enemies of his friends would speak a word against him.

In the carriage returning home, I drifted off listening to our mothers speculating whether one who was so well-connected as Colonel Petrov might ever deign to take a bride with little to offer.

"With no family to please, he may indulge his own whim."

"He could do better."

"Of course. But there is no law written for fools. Consider the match that Count Sheremetev made for his youngest son last year. She brought nothing but a few sticks of furniture and a pleasing face."

Once home, I followed Xenia and Nadya to our room at a drowsy distance. Nadya was in a fury, pulling ribbons and combs from her hair and leaving a trail of these obstacles in the darkened passage. "You think only of yourself," I heard her accuse Xenia. "You set your eye on some drunkard, and when he does not ask you to dance, you make a fool of yourself and spoil both our chances."

I mewled for Olga to undress me and put me to bed, but she did not heed me.

"What is this, kitten?" she asked Nadya.

Nadya brushed her off like a flea from her bosom and squared off to Xenia. "Admit it. You did it on purpose."

Xenia did not deny the charge. "I only rearranged the order to put us with our right partners."

"Right partners!"

"I am going to marry him."

It irked Nadya beyond endurance when Xenia said things she could not possibly know. "Spare me your drivel. He was amusing himself with you, and you are the only one who did not see it. And what of me? I suppose I am to marry the old man you stuck me with?"

"Yes."

Nadya sneered. "And how shall you explain this to his wife and children?"

Xenia shook her head, puzzled. "I do not know."

ON A DAY IN APRIL, some months after the Empress's ball, the house was made ready—we did not know for what, only that the floors were being scrubbed, the carpets beaten, and each window polished inside and out. Lyuba could not be bothered to make our breakfast, and we were given only bread, after which Olga took us to the banya that we might also be scrubbed. It was not our customary day for bathing, and we were eaten by curiosity to find the cause for all this. Olga only shook her head. "Someone is coming to dine, but that is all I shall say."

"He must be someone of importance," Nadya prodded. "Is it Uncle Kolya's commander?"

Olga gave a look that said she knew well enough but not even the torments of the rack would loosen her tongue. "You will know soon."

"It is your husband," Xenia said to Nadya.

So far as I knew, our mothers had not yet narrowed to a single person the possible candidates for Nadya's hand. Still, had Xenia said that the moon was a pancake, I should have believed her.

"How do you know?" Nadya demanded.

"I dreamt last night that an egg rolled in the door. Lyuba picked it up and was going to use it for a cake, but then she gave it to you instead."

"What piddle!" Nadya said, but she was pale.

Though most of Xenia's dreams had no more relation to our lives than a hand does to a sack of grain, on some few occasions a remembered dream of hers had replayed itself in our waking lives. Once, she had dreamt of a hare, and the next day a hare had come onto the path where we were walking. It stopped, rose up on its hind legs, and in the manner of a person who sees someone on the street he thinks he may know, it looked at us briefly before springing away. Another time, she dreamt of someone drowning, and a week later a boy in the village fell into the river and was lost. As Nadya had said, even a blind pig finds an acorn once in a while. Or maybe it was only that Xenia was more attentive to all the minute shifts and eddies in the atmosphere that pass beneath the notice of others—a rustle in the grass, a whisper in the servants' hall.

Whatever the explanation, Aunt Galya came to our room later that day to oversee our dressing for dinner and instructed Olga to change Nadya's skirt.

"There is someone coming whom I'm anxious you should impress."

Outside, there was the rattle of an approaching carriage and horses, and with it the baying of hounds. Aunt Galya sprang to the door. "Nadya, hurry," she scolded, as though Nadya had been dawdling. "We mustn't keep him waiting."

From the window, we watched the carriage clatter into the courtyard, trailed by a roiling pack of dogs. A footman leapt down, opened the carriage's door, and with difficulty helped to extricate its contents. The low door and narrow step from the carriage necessitated a hazardous shifting and resettling of the occupant's considerable girth, but once he was aright and rebalanced on his spindly legs, we saw it was the elderly gentleman with whom Nadya had danced at the ball. He made his slow way to the door and was lost to our view.

"Stop looking at me," Nadya hissed, and when this had no effect, "You don't know a thing. You cannot." She bit her lip, turned, and ran after Aunt Galya.

My father and the egg-shaped gentleman were taking their leisure in front of the stove, and after they had finished their vodka we all retired to the dining room and took our customary places round the table, excepting Nadya, who was seated directly across from our guest that he might have an unimpeded view of her. His glass was filled first, and then my father lifted his own.

"My family is honored by your presence, Kuzma Zakharovich. In your long service at court, you must have dined in very auspicious company."

"What's that?"

"I'm honored, sir, to have you at my table."

The good man nodded absently and began to eat, freeing us to follow. At first, I kept my eyes on my plate, stealing only occasional glances by first lifting my napkin to my lips, but each time I looked, Kuzma Zakharovich was so intent on his food that I shortly dispensed with the subterfuge. He worked at the meat, his lower lip thrusting out wetly and then receding, thrusting and receding, and his jowls rolling like a ship in heavy swells. Stopping to wet the mess with a slurp of wine, he then continued until, with a final effort, he swallowed the morsel.

My father was not himself a man given to easy conversation. He tested various themes without success before he hit upon the solitary enthusiasm of Kuzma Zakharovich beyond his digestion.

"Have you had good hunting this season?"

The gentleman's countenance brightened visibly. "At Peterhof this past month, the Empress's guests shot three

hundred and twelve fowl. A goodly number of them wild
geese."

Between mouthfuls of soup and eggs and pickled cabbage, Kuzma Zakharovich privileged the table with an accounting of various takes, divided by the quantities of each
species, and, further, by the individual tallies of each member of the party.

"  . . . of these, Count Betsky shot sixty-eight." Kuzma
Zakharovich paused, allowing us to digest this number and
himself a spoonful of mushrooms. "Twenty-seven of them
quail," he added. "However, the official tally counted only
twenty-three, as four were winged and not recovered."

What would it be to sit at breakfast and dinner for the
rest of one's days and listen to a droning recitation of favored personages and the creatures that had fallen for their
sport? I watched with horrified fascination a bit of bread
wobbling on his lower lip.

"  . . . of course, these numbers are nothing as compared
with those of our dear reposed Empress." Kuzma Zakharovich's eyes grew rheumy.

The late Empress Anna Ioannovna had been a devoted
huntress—she was said to keep loaded guns at various posts
throughout the palace so that she might walk down a corridor and shoot at gulls through the windows—and it was she
who had made Kuzma Zakharovich Grand Master of the
Hunt. So continually had he been at her side—praising her
aim and advising her how she might stock her parks next
season with tigers from Siberia or peacocks from India—
that he was widely thought to have her ear. As a conse-

quence, his company had been sought after and endured, and his first marriage to a niece of Count Peter Saltykov had excited much envy.

His star had fallen somewhat since then: Anna Ioan-novna had died, and the new Empress preferred dancing to shooting. Her Imperial Majesty Elizabeth had replaced him as Grand Master with her own Count Razumovsky, who was, according to Kuzma Zakharovich, an indifferent hunter. And now Kuzma Zakharovich's wife had died in childbirth. But as he said, the Lord had provided comfort for this most recent loss: she had left behind not only a newborn son but six other children as well.

With the mention of his wife and children, his gaze turned to rest on Nadya with the dispassion of a man judging the weight of a doe.

"Does she ride?"

"She has had little opportunity," my father answered, "but she is teachable."

"Well, no matter," Kuzma Zakharovich conceded. "She seems in all other ways adequate."

With that, our part in the matter was concluded. We were excused so that the gentlemen might discuss the terms of the contract and fix a date for the betrothal dinner.

When the door closed behind us, Mother and Aunt Galya began to chatter about Nadya's marvelous good fortune.

Nadya herself did not see it.

"You are too innocent to know your own luck, lamb," Aunt Galya said. "Old men make the best husbands. They are not forever coming to your bed with their needs and when they do, they are more easily satisfied. And think, he has no mother to rule you. You should count yourself lucky."

"But he is dull," Nadya objected.

Aunt Galya dismissed her. "He is rich."

Nadya lifted her head a little. "Is he?"

"Two hundred a year. This in addition to the first wife's dowry village. And he is on familiar terms with persons of influence."

Nadya was brought round to recognize the advantages in becoming Kuzma Zakharovich's wife. Not the least of the persuasions was the silvered hand mirror he presented to her at the betrothal dinner.

IT WAS TO THE BENEFIT of Xenia that never before or since has the Russian court been so musical. Empress Elizabeth Petrovna's was the reign of song. On Monday afternoons, there was dance music, on Wednesdays, Italian compositions, and on Tuesdays and Thursdays, musical comedies. The evenings were taken up variously with allegories composed in Her Imperial Majesty's honor, an opera, or the newest play from France. An army of artisans—playwrights and musicians, seamstresses and carpenters—worked by lamplight late into the nights penning and producing new amusements. Companies of dancers and singers, got up in folk costumes and dancing the mazurka one day, were swirling about the stage the next, swathed in the filmy attire of gods and goddesses. At any or all of these entertainments, the members of the court choir might perform, with Colonel Petrov numbered among them.

Our mothers could not gain her entry to the more exclusive amusements of the court, but Xenia became a devotee of the public concerts. She came home after these elated or dejected, depending on whether Colonel Petrov had sung.

How long could it have been before he noticed her, there in every audience and so clearly listening only to him? His eyes met hers and his mouth bowed slightly, not quite a smile but enough for Xenia. He sought her out at the end of the concert, and in the aftermath the exchange between them was studied like egg whites.

"Did you note how solicitous he was of Xenia?" my mother said. "He asked twice if she enjoyed the concert."

"He likes to be flattered," Aunt Galya answered. "It is one thing to be agreeable, daughter, and another to be so eager. You should not give the impression that his attentions matter overly much."

"But they do." Xenia said this so simply that Aunt Galya could only sigh and shake her head.

"All the more reason then to be circumspect until you know his intentions."

My mother intervened. "There's no need, Galya. These two are berries from the same field. When I let it drop that we sometimes stroll in the Summer Garden, he asked straight out if we would be there tomorrow."

"You told him yes?" Xenia was desperate.

"I said that we might stroll in the morning, provided it did not rain."

It didn't rain and he was there, circling about at the palace entrance. He asked that he might call at the house, and before the day was out he had proposed marriage. Though this relieved our mothers of the burden of feigning happenstance, they had still to slow the galloping pace of the young lovers for the sake of appearances.

I remember one more such afternoon in the garden. Xenia and Andrei were strolling together, and as is the custom during the betrothal, others were in attendance: my mother and aunt, myself and Nadya, and a few other women of our acquaintance who enjoyed being included in the periphery of any courtship. The young couple walked a short distance ahead of their entourage, and this was all the privacy they would be allowed until the wedding night.

Andrei and Xenia were so entirely absorbed by each other that they walked the long avenues without stopping, undiverted by statues or fountains or other whimsies. We in pursuit also made only cursory note of them, watching instead the pantomime before us. Out of earshot, Andrei inclined his head into the space between himself and Xenia and spoke in low tones. We could not hear his words, but such looks of ardor passed from him to her, and even his bearing bespoke the constraints on his liberty. Xenia returned his rapt gaze and nodded in eager agreement to each of his utterances, and this seemed to feed his fervor all the more.

Later, Aunt Galya quizzed Xenia. "What was said between you?"

"He instructed me on the superiority of partes singing."

"And what else?"

"That is all."

Apparently, Andrei Feodorovich was quite passionate on the innovation that had come from his native Kiev.
Xenia repeated his claim that man was not intended by
God to sing all in unison. Just as Christ was both human
and divine, the lower voice in partes singing represents the
earthly, and the higher voice embodies the spiritual. The
ancient chants would deny the physical by bending all reg-
isters to one sound. Not so in partes. The two voices each
sing their own nature, and the sounds they make when they
come together are rapturous and complete. The physical
becomes spiritual. Or so was his explanation.

There was something in this our mothers did not quite
approve, but they had no talent to parse such a difficult
theological argument. "I am not, after all, a student of
church music," Aunt Galya said.

However, Xenia understood his meaning well enough.
She whispered to me later, "I think he would teach me to
sing in his bed."

AT THE CLOSE OF SUMMER, Grand Duke Peter wed our present Empress, Catherine. A week following the Imperial
wedding, Nadya was married, and a fortnight after this,
Xenia followed suit.

*That He will bless this marriage, as He blessed the marriage in
Cana of Galilee, let us pray to the Lord.*

*Lord have mercy.*

There is a cathedral, wan light falling in dusty shafts

from so high up that it dies before reaching the stony depths. There, in the dimness flecked with a thousand candles, a crowd waves like grasses on the floor of a sea. Attached to this impression is the sweetish smell of beeswax and incense and warm bodies. The bee buzz of the crowd.

This is most certainly the Cathedral of Kazan, where the Grand Duke and Duchess wed, for my cousins and their grooms would not have merited such a buzz.

*Did you note his condescension to Count Razumovsky?*

A woman with a long white face and reddened lips directs her comment to a dowager whose crepey bosom rests atop her corset like two wrinkled peaches. The older woman answers something, but I cannot hear what.

*That He will make them glad in the beholding of sons and daughters, let us pray to the Lord.*

*Ah, well, rooster today, feather duster tomorrow.*

*Lord, have mercy.*

Strange that I cannot entirely tease apart which impression belongs to which day. Perhaps it is that every wedding is so much the same—such endless repetitions and circlings are required to make two persons one. But the more likely explanation is this: though marriage was the end towards which we'd been unspooling since birth, I was stunned by the arrival of it. There is no word in the language to denote being orphaned of sisters by marriage. Did it exist, it would describe my inchoate and confused emotions. Even Nadya's leaving was so peculiarly painful to me that I recoiled from feeling the greater loss of Xenia. I pretended poorly to the general happiness.

Over the immense royal doors behind the altar, Christ is enthroned and is judging the proceedings. He is flanked by a solemn jury of saints—John the Baptist, Theotokis, the archangels Gabriel and Michael, the apostles Peter and Paul. Thin feet hang beneath their rigid robes; their long fingers gesture stiffly. Their impassive countenances suggest that though they pity the dwarfed creatures below, their thoughts are elsewhere. In orderly rows, their elongated figures tower up and up towards heaven.

*That He will grant them and us all our petitions which are for salvation, let us pray to the Lord.*

A priest stands beneath the saints. In his stiff-collared stole and miter, he resembles one of their number come to life. He presides with equanimity over the stumbling flock that comes before him in endless, faceless pairs to be joined. Taking their hands into his, he asks them if they wish to have one another and to live together. He asks thrice.

*Be exalted, O Bridegroom, like unto Abraham.*

*He hardly looks the part of the joyous groom.*

*Do you of a good free and uncoerced will and with good intention take to yourself as wife this woman whom you see here before you?*

Kuzma Zakharovich, I see him now, pondering the lit candle grasped in his fat fingers. He turns his face to the priest before him and then to the girl beside him, with the muddled look of a man who finds himself placed in an awkward position.

*Do you of a good free and uncoerced will and with good intention take to yourself as wife this woman whom you see here before you?*

The Grand Duke's demeanor is even more strikingly discordant. Though dressed like a monarch, he has the sallow appearance of a sickly child. His recent illness has left him horribly pocked and plucked-looking. He slouches in boyish defiance, makes faces, answers the priest in petulant tones, and pretends to a haughty boredom that he cannot pull off. Every twitch betrays him, as though the clothes are too heavy.

The priest places the crowns upon their heads, he holds out the goblet with the warm red wine for them to drink, and he leads them thrice round the altar table. He beseeches Christ and the saints to bless their goings out and their comings in, and to bless their union with fruitfulness, to increase their numbers.

*Bride, be exalted like unto Sarah; and exult, like unto Rebecca: and multiply, like unto Rachel.*

Happy and delighted—such words are too much employed for frivolous emotions. The bride is called to be exultant. Xenia has such a look. Her profile is radiant, she is so entranced by her beloved that she might be on an island and he the only other inhabitant. She is very far away.

*And rejoice in your husband, fulfilling the conditions of the law: for so is it well-pleasing unto God.*

Tears are streaming down my cheeks.

Of Nadya, my only memory is the moment when the priest placed the wedding crown upon her head. It might have been made of thorns. I watch her lift her chin slightly, her throat pulling into taut lines. Her features, set in an attitude of resignation, stiffen. And then she reaches up with one hand to straighten the crown on her hair, and I gasp, thinking of grain clattering onto the floor.

But no, this must be the Grand Duchess, after all, for the sleeve that lifts to adjust the crown is of richly embroidered silver cloth and is slit open to reveal a lining of white swan's down.

*Replenish their life with good things. Receive their crowns into Thy kingdom, preserving them spotless, blameless, and without reproach, unto ages of ages.*

Afterwards, in a shower of hemp seed, Xenia ducks her head into Andrei's shoulder, and he covers her protectively. I am bereft. When the wedding party tries to pull apart the bride and groom, I forget the spirit of the game and tug at Xenia with childish, heartsick ferocity. Dazed with joy and clinging to Andrei, she smiles straight through me.

Later, her bridal sheets are brought to the wedding banquet and hung so all can see the bloody stains on them. A cheer goes up, and there is much laughter. Love is brutal.

## CHAPTER FOUR

I am conscious that I have violated a tradition of story-telling: a wedding shall signal the happy close to a tale. At this moment, any couple may yet stand in for every other; they are the blank slate on which are chalked our hopeful expectations.

What comes after the wedding, this is the province of nurses and mothers. They lay bare the mystery with commonplaces. Love and eggs are best when they are fresh. The wife who invites her husband to visit her while she is dressing invites his eventual disinterest. Take your thoughts to bed with you, they intone, for the morning is wiser than the evening.

For all this common wisdom, though, the heart of each particular marriage remains hidden. While sorting my mother's effects after her death, I found the packet of letters my father had sent her so many years earlier from the front. They bore no relation to the heartsick professions Nadya had improvised in our games but were, instead, the most conventional of exchanges concerning the progress of the war and the management of my father's estate and household. Try as I might, I could parse no feeling in them. Each was signed "Your husband, Nikolai Feodosievich," as though she might not otherwise have known him. And yet she kept these letters until the end of her days. I am desirous to think that my mother and father may yet have loved each other, but their true feelings were so commingled with obligation that it is impossible to know. My father would not have known even how to frame such a question. He was a soldier and hence disposed to thinking not in terms of affection but only in terms of duty.

For her part, my mother was probably more alike him than he suspected, the chief difference being that showing her husband affection was among her duties. Though she might harshly reprimand a servant or child, in his presence she was always soft-spoken and demure. She deferred to his opinions, flattered his vanities, and endured his rebukes with meekness. Love was a choice she made, and then made again daily for the remainder of her life. From her I learnt that a woman should not expect her happiness to come from the man himself, but from those acts of devotion she showed to him.

NADYA DID NOT LEARN THIS lesson. As Aunt Galya had predicted, Kuzma Zakharovich demanded little of her, but she found married life trying nonetheless. Chief amongst her complaints was Kuzma Zakharovich's eldest daughter, at seventeen only two years younger than Nadya herself.

"She conspires to turn my husband against me," Nadya

complained. "She even allows the servants to be insolent. I ring and ring and no one will bring my coffee. They pretend they do not hear me, but I am ringing loudly enough."

Nadya even insisted that the girl was trying to kill her. Her proof of this charge was that the daughter had insisted on cooking mutton in the house though Nadya was by then expecting a child and the smells of food made her ill. When the baby came, Nadya claimed to see Kuzma Zakharovich's daughter give the infant the evil eye. "She denied it, of course, but I know what I saw. If this child dies, it will be on her head."

Kuzma Zakharovich declined to be drawn into these quarrels and went hunting instead. Nor could Nadya find a sympathetic ear in her own family. Her mother emptily counseled patience, a game for which Nadya had no talent. More maddening, her own sister could not even be made to see the difficulty. Xenia could not conceive that one whom God had blessed with a mate might have any cause to be discontented. Nadya retorted that Xenia would not be so blithe had God dealt *her* Kuzma Zakharovich and his daughter. "Your happiness blinds you to the suffering of others."

It was true that Xenia seemed uniquely blessed in her match. Andrei treated her with tenderness, and she returned his affection with adoration. A mention of him was sufficient to make her eyes soften, and if he was in the room, though she might seem engaged in conversation and give the outward appearance of attention, I could see that she was wholly preoccupied with him and he with her as well. Without a glance, much less a word or touch, they vibrated as though an invisible string stretched taut between them.

He spoilt her by buying for her whatever thing she fancied, with no eye to the cost. When she admired in passing Anna Vorontsovskaya's Chinese fan, he ordered a copy made for her. Her delight in this gift so pleased him that after this he was continually looking for some new thing that should please her. She returned his extravagance. That Andrei might be proud of his table, she stocked the larder with rich foods—ducks and cheeses and kegs of beer—and their house became known for its hospitality. That he might be proud of her as well, she gave attention to her dress and hair. Once, he failed to compliment her on a new skirt and bodice, and at last she got it from him that he did not like her as much in muted hues. It was a beautiful dress, moiré silk the color of dried lavender, but no matter. She gave it straightaway to me and had another made just like it but in bright yellow.

Because it was her nature to be generous, she was intent that I, too, should know this happiness. As yet, no one had shown an inclination to deprive my family of me. My mother and aunt reasoned that a sixteen-year-old had two or three more seasons of bloom yet, but they did not seem hopeful of my prospects. Xenia took it upon herself to find me a husband. She applied to this task all her customary energies, attaching me to guest lists, lending me dresses from her wardrobe, and counseling me. Once, when I expressed a desire to stay home, she said, "Once you are married, you need never go out again. But if you will only pretend to a little gaiety tonight, perhaps you will feel it, too."

We were going that evening to the home of Leonid Vladimirovich Berevsky. In his day, he kept an open house where anyone might come and dine at his table, and on a given evening he might feed the Empress and fifty of her courtiers or no one at all. His chef was famously inventive, for one supper creating a flotilla of ships carved from pineapples, for another decorating cakes with trellises of spun sugar and candied violets. Many went there only to sample what new novelty would be presented.

That evening we were served a dish of roast suckling pig stuffed with quails, these in turn stuffed with mushrooms. Leonid Vladimirovich's daughter sat at table with her little pug dog seated on a chair next to her. Eufimia, short-limbed and fat, bore an unhappy resemblance to the bug-eyed little beast, a likeness she had witlessly enhanced by dressing the dog in a collar of the same gold lace that trimmed her own bodice.

"He is very clever," Eufimia said. "Observe this." Pulling the leg off a quail, she held the tiny drumstick just above the dog's nose. "Didi, demonstrate how Mademoiselle Talyzina danced the mazurka at court." She waggled the drumstick just out of its reach, and it rose onto its hind legs, tottering and spinning. Everyone laughed and applauded. Someone hummed a tune to accompany the dog, and others began to call out the names of various persons for Didi to imitate.

Count Razumovsky whispered, "Would that the mistress had the charms of her pet." I could think of no witty answer but smiled encouragingly. Gospodin Chogalovsky on my left repeated the remark to the person on his left and I watched it circle the table, a discreet whisper, a titter, a shared glance, until it reached Xenia. Inclining her head towards her neighbor, she listened, but her fierce eyes remained fixed on the dog. By now, it was wheezing desperately from its exertions. It collapsed onto its haunches but then struggled back up when Eufimia dangled the drumstick in front of its nose.

Xenia rose. "May I try?" she asked Eufimia. She waited, holding out a hand.

Reluctantly, Eufimia passed her the drumstick. "Hold it just above his snout," she instructed.

"Like so?" Xenia held out the drumstick but so low that the dog lunged and snatched a bit of greasy meat from the bone. She feigned surprise and dropped the drumstick to the floor, whereupon the dog fell off its chair and began to devour it.

"Oh, dear." She could not keep from laughing. "Good boy, Didi! Look with what relish he enjoys his meat."

"I can't think who he puts me in mind of," said Gospodin Chogalovsky. Someone volunteered the name of an Austrian attaché with famously bad table manners.

"Yes, that's him exactly!"

The game turned to one in which Didi was encouraged to eat in the manner of various people we did not like. Scraps of food were tossed on the floor, and the dog happily snuffled them up.

Eufimia pouted. "No, make him dance." She held up another drumstick but could no longer engage her dog's attention.

One of Eufimia's several suitors—she might be unattractive, but she stood to inherit much charm—volunteered that he would happily dance if he might feed from her hand. With a simper, Eufimia held up the drumstick and requested the figures of a sarabande. He obliged, to more laughter. Such was the nature of our amusement most evenings.

ANDREI, BEING ATTACHED TO THE court, was compelled to move in its seasonal cycles, quitting Petersburg in the spring for more hospitable climates. From Petersburg to Moscow, to Oranienbaum and the summer palace at Tsarskoye Selo, to monasteries and country estates and back again—the Empress was a restless traveler, and wherever she went an endless line of carriages and carts snaked behind her carrying all her furniture and her several thousand dresses and shoes, and behind them her vast retinue, often nearly a quarter of the populace of Petersburg, a moveable city of pilgrims journeying endlessly from shrine to shrine, seeking some new diversion.

Because Xenia could not bear to be apart from her husband, she often numbered amongst these travelers. Even I, who had no relation to the court, was brought along on one such journey, an Imperial pilgrimage to Lake Svetloyar. Xenia had arranged it. A pilgrimage, she reasoned, would provide opportunities for informal meetings and conversation. And I should not have to dance.

The court left Tsarskoye Selo after the roads were dry and traveled first to Prince Merchersky's estate near Nizhny Novgorod. After a week of the Prince's hospitality, the vast machine of the Empress's retinue set out on foot for the lake.

Within two hours of our departing, word came back through the line that Her Imperial Majesty was fatigued. We were compelled to stop then and there and await carriages to convey us the remaining nine or ten versts to our lodgings. The next day, the carriages returned us to the exact spot where we had previously left off, and we continued walking from there. That afternoon, we made little more progress before the Empress suffered a blister on her heel. Again, we waited for carriages to shuttle us forward in small groups, a tedious process that took longer than it would have to walk the same distance. And so it went. Each day, the carriages deposited us on this same stretch of road and then picked us up again some incremental distance farther on. It was three days before we passed our lodgings on foot and four days before the tail of the line accomplished this same feat.

Xenia did not forget her purpose in bringing me along, and contrived each day to put us in the company of various unattached men. Into the second week, we stood one afternoon by the side of the road watching the procession of pilgrims pass, until she spotted a page she had met the previous evening. My first thought was that Xenia had misjudged: I had seen this same young man seated at supper next to one of the Shuvalov brothers.

"Yes, he is their nephew," she answered.

"He is too far above me." I did not add that he was too pretty as well.

"The heart does not know its station."

She took me by the arm and fell in just ahead of the page. When he caught sight of her, she expressed delight at the happy accident of meeting again.

"This is my cousin Daria Nikolayevna of whom I spoke. Dasha, this is Ivan Ivanovich. He is a great lover of books. I told him last evening that you read."

He expressed his pleasure at making my acquaintance and asked if I might commend any books to him. I had read the whole of what was available to me—the Psalter, the domestic rules of the *Domostroi*, and a pamphlet condemning the aggressions of the former King of Sweden—in short, nothing I might recommend. I returned the question. He recommended a book of lives by a Roman called Plutarch and described to me its virtues. He then kindly offered to lend me his volume.

Had we more time, we might have gotten on well, for he was frank and intelligent and fond of ideas. But our walk was cut short by a pebble in the Empress's slipper.

We did not see Ivan Ivanovich again over the next several days. After Xenia asked Andrei to make inquiries, we learnt that the page had been moved to the head of the procession and was now walking in the company of the Empress herself.

"I fear the Shuvalovs have designs for him." Andrei was grim. It seemed the brothers, dangerous and tireless schemers both, had brought their nephew on the pilgrimage with the purpose of introducing him to the Empress. By all appearances, they had calculated rightly the particular weakness of their sovereign. This young man, twenty-seven years her junior, had caught the Empress's fancy, and the enemies of Razumovsky were gleefully predicting that the Count would be out on his ear soon.

Andrei reflected the gradual darkening of the courtiers' mood. The lake lay no more than one hundred and twenty versts to the east of our starting point, but it had taken us nearly a fortnight to cover half that distance, for we could walk at best an hour a day before Her Majesty became winded or footsore. Prince Merchersky remarked that the early fathers might never have made it to the Holy Land had they been obliged to wear corsets and slippers. It began to seem we should be on that road forever, and the prospect bred a restive ill-temper which spread like disease in the close quarters. However various were our lodgings en route, they shared the quality of being overcrowded. Xenia and I were compelled one night to lie in a doorsill and were woken a dozen times by people stepping over us. On another night, we slept seated in a long queue of carriages parked before the inn where the Empress and her ladies were bedded.

Xenia, however, remained cheerful. She liked being out of doors and relished every aspect of travel. As we walked, each new prospect excited her, though its only virtue might seem to be that it was unfamiliar. Even the small hardships, she insisted cheerily, were a diversion from one's daily routines and familiar discomforts. Why, she might even become a wandering monk. Andrei replied that she would make a terrible monk. "How would you manage without your dresses and baubles? Besides, you have no gift for being alone." She snugged her arm into the crook of his and said that he was right. Though she could live without her worldly possessions, she would die if deprived of his company.

At last our caravan reached the lake. There being no suitable lodgings in the vicinity, scores of tents had been erected in a meadow overlooking the water. Our spirits were lifted to have finally reached our destination and to find it equal to all that had been said of it. The lake, glassy and round as a mirror, looked like a circle cut from the sky and set down there. Cottony clouds floated on the still blue surface, and lily pads and cattails garlanded the rim. Andrei jested that the city of Kitezh had risen again.

The legend goes that five hundred years ago, a city of golden-domed churches stood there. This was in the time of Batu Khan, when his barbarous warriors swarmed across the land, setting fire to every village and town, slaying without mercy old men and mothers, and sweeping up children onto the backs of their horses to be sold into slavery. Even the great Kiev was laid waste, its churches and libraries burnt, its streets turned to rivers of blood, and not a single person spared to mourn the dead. Then Batu Khan turned his army towards the city of Kitezh. In anticipation of the coming terror, the people built no fortifications and made no preparations to defend their city but instead prayed fervently to God to spare them.

It is said that as the Mongol horde approached the walls of the city, fountains of water sprouted from the ground around them. Khan's army retreated and watched from a remove as God caused the city to be swallowed into a deep lake.

Many pilgrim to Lake Svetloyar to pray and to drink from these waters. Holy persons have sometimes reported seeing the lights of the invisible city glimmering in the black depths or hearing, faintly, the tolling of bells and the murmured prayers of the ancient inhabitants. There are even stories of pilgrims who have gone there and never returned, or they have disappeared for a time and then reappeared on the banks of the lake with no memory of where they have been.

That evening, we processed down to the water, where hundreds of candles had been set adrift and twinkled in the summer dusk. We knelt in the damp grasses and turned to watch Her Imperial Majesty take the final steps of the pilgrimage. On her left was Count Razumovsky and close by, Ivan Ivanovich Shuvalov. At the edge of the water, Razumovsky helped the Empress to kneel onto a carpet. Her confessor said the prayers and then, dipping a goblet into the lake, held it for her to drink. When she had drunk, she held a plump hand out, not to Razumovsky but to Ivan Ivanovich. He handed her onto her throne, which had been carried from Petersburg, and she rested her tired feet on a stool.

Across the dark water came the high note of a hand bell, icy and ethereal. Then another bell and another, and beneath these sounds, a slow, upwelling chant. The hum of whispers occasioned by Her Imperial Majesty's slighting of her favorite fell away, and all eyes turned towards the water. The Empress had commissioned a song to be written for the occasion of our arrival. I knew that Andrei, with the choir, was installed on a barge tethered somewhere off the shore to sing it, but peering into the gloaming I could not discern the source of the music. It was as though a fissure had opened up, sonorous and deep, and was breathing out the sounds of the ancient city, and the even more ancient sounds of the earth itself. Whales and beetles, grass pushing up through the soil, the slow exhalation of mountains and tides, the buzz of everything, living or not, swelling and contracting and pulling the soul down into its music.

A chorus of supplications rose to the heavens. Save us, O merciful Lord, they sang, in this our time of trouble. And the waters began to rise and to turn back the barbarians, who fell away in fear and awe. The waters filled the streets and crept up the walls of the houses, rising above the roofs, and still the voices could be heard praising God. One by one, the domes of the many churches disappeared until the Mongol's last sight of the city was a gold cross hovering above the water. The voice of the choir grew triumphant. It extolled the long line of holy ones from Kitezh to our present mother, Elizabeth, whose prayers had sheltered Russia from its enemies. At the end of time, the choir sang, this golden-domed city would rise up again, a new kingdom on earth. The hand bells accompanying the choir rang out and then died. We on the banks strained to hear the last tones melting into the silence.

As the choir sang, Xenia had clasped my hand hard. Tears had shone in her eyes, and they had a bright, ecstatic look. Now, the courtiers stirred to life and began to talk amongst themselves, but she remained still and as vacant in aspect as one in a trance.

"The choir sang as I have never heard them," I said to her.

She did not answer, though she was usually happy to hear the choir praised, making no distinction between this and praise of Andrei in particular. People hurried past us, heading back up the rise to where a supper had been laid on long tables in the open air. At long last, like a person returning from a great distance, she blinked and her eyes took in her surroundings.

"The choir sang as I have never heard them," I repeated. Still caught in reverie, she nodded.

She was uncommonly quiet for the remainder of the evening, and not even Andrei's merriness roused her from her distraction. He expressed concern that the journey had overtaxed her. "Are you unwell?" he asked.

"No, no, I am fine. It is . . ." She scanned the air for more words but did not find them. "Do you not feel it?"

"What?"

"That our lives are shadows. You, me, all this, it does not mean a thing."

He was at a loss how to answer.

"No, that sounds horrible, I am not expressing it well.

What if the lake, the trees, the heavens, everything we can see, is a forgery, like painted scenery? Lovely as it is, what if it is not real and there is something else?"

With a little shake of her head, she fell back into silence. She was quiet and more distractible the next day, but she gradually returned to herself once we had left Lake Svetloyar and come home again.

# The Metamorphoses Ball

## CHAPTER FIVE

With each passing season, my father grew less willing to assume the expenses attendant on my being out in society, and my prospects dimmed a little further. I can fix no moment when expectation gave way to anxiety. Where once I had wondered at intervals whether the husband in my future might be kind or cruel, as the years passed I found myself thinking less about his character and fearing only that he might not exist. It was akin to awaiting the arrival of a distant guest to a party: in the whirl of other guests, his absence may not even register at first, and when it is noted, there is perhaps only a slight vexation at the person's lateness. But as time goes on, this vexation changes to apprehension and then distress, until his absence casts a longer shadow than his presence might ever command.

In the winter of my twentieth year, the matter came to a head. At the same time that my brother went into the Guards, my father was retired from it. Freed from his service to the crown, he was now able to remove his family from the city and live out his remaining years on his own land.

Going with them would settle my fate—my father's estate was on the Kashinka River, six days' journey from Moscow, and there were no eligible men in the vicinity. Aunt Galya proposed that I stay behind with her under the roof of her elder daughter. I cannot guess whether my aunt had anticipated Nadya's answer when she made the suggestion, but Nadya was indignant. She had already to contend with Kuzma Zakharovich's wretched daughter and her own mother, and now she should take in a cousin as well? Her sister had no burdens, she countered; why should not Xenia do her share?

Andrei and Xenia showed great kindness in making me welcome, even insisting that it was I who would be doing them a service by keeping Xenia company when she could not travel with Andrei. And so, I went to live with them.

My things were sent ahead, and when I arrived, I learnt that she had put my bed in the upstairs room next to hers. This room had been kept unfurnished in expectation of children. Now, the door stood open, and I saw beyond the threshold that a curtain had been made for the window, my personal linens were already unpacked in the wardrobe, and the icon that had guarded my sleep since birth hung in the corner. I demurred, saying that I should be content to sleep with the servants, but Xenia shook off my protests.

"Nonsense. If it's bad luck to buy the cradle before the child, maybe it's just as bad to keep a room empty." Her manner was so easy that I didn't guess at the time what this kindness must have cost her.

The first year of their marriage had passed without any sign of a child, and then a year became two and then three. In the fourth year, she had got with child but her womb would not hold it and it was lost before it quickened. She rarely spoke of her disappointment, but after I moved into their house I came to sense that it was never far from her thoughts. She kept in her room a little icon of Saint Paraskeva, who gives children to barren women, and a candle was kept lit before it. Each month, when her blood came, she was prone to tears over the littlest things.

The Imperial family was also waiting on the Grand Duchess to produce an heir for the throne. From the start of their marriage, the Empress had insisted that the ducal couple should be locked together in their bedchamber each night, like prisoners, so that they might get a child. One of Catherine's ladies-in-waiting whispered that in this enforced privacy, Peter spent all night playing with his tin soldiers, lining them up in formation across the wide plain of their bed and engaging them in mock battles, or sawing on his violin whilst the Grand Duchess tried to sleep.

As time ticked on, the Empress was observed to be increasingly impatient and irritable towards her. She accused Catherine of conducting an affair and set spies on her to report her every move. The Grand Duke, meanwhile, showed no interest in his wife and flirted openly with the Princess of Courland, who was hideous and seemed to have nothing to recommend her save that she would speak in German with him.

It was rumored that in the end Her Majesty had given

up and looked the other way so that Catherine might take a lover. Shortly after, she was with child. Rumors were thick that Sergei Saltykov was the father. If true, the child's parentage became moot, for in May Catherine miscarried whilst traveling. Though she had made every effort to please her husband and her Empress, this grave failure could not be offset by any amount of charm.

Of course, I was not privy to any of this directly but heard it through Xenia, who heard it from I know not whom. Xenia felt a heightened sympathy for the Grand Duchess, and took Her Highness's sorrow as her own. Every conversation turned to the loss of this child and would end in tears. The Grand Duchess's circumstances merited sympathy, certainly, but hardly so extreme a response; in truth, I felt she became a bit tiresome on the subject.

We were dining one evening at the house of one of the Roslavlev brothers, a captain in the Izmailovsky Guards, and the buzz about the table concerned a Mademoiselle Shavirova, one of Catherine's ladies-in-waiting, who was thought to be the Grand Duke's most recent infatuation. That afternoon and in the presence of the Grand Duchess, the two of them had sat with their heads bowed together and giggled through most of the concert.

It is safe to say that no one at the table cared for the Grand Duke, but though tongues were loosened by a good deal of wine, they were not so loose as to say a word outright against him. Instead, their mirth was directed at the mademoiselle, who was, it was agreed, the least attractive of the Grand Duchess's ladies. Someone ventured the opinion that love could not possibly be this blind. Another agreed that it was not love but spite against Catherine for her attentions to Saltykov.

This is the way of life in Petersburg—even the lowliest person in society watches the court from whatever his distance and follows the rivalries and intrigues like a sporting match— but Xenia could not treat the gossip as mere diversion. When someone at the table said that the Grand Duke must surely be deprived of his wife's affection if he sought solace from such a toad, Xenia spoke as if she were defending her own honor.

"Does this not better prove that his wife is deprived of a child through no fault of her own?" She clutched her napkin so fiercely that her hand shook.

The hour was late when we left, and we had all drunk too much. The three of us stumbled into the dim interior of the hired carriage, and Xenia and I plucked pillows from beneath our skirts and fashioned little nests for our heads. Andrei slouched onto the opposite bench and was lost up to the waist beneath the foamy horizon of our skirts. As soon as I was off my feet, I was overcome by the groggy weight of my limbs. Reaching above my head, Andrei opened the pane of the carriage lamp and blew out the flame. The carriage's interior disappeared.

I let my eyes close. The carriage lurched forward, and behind my lids the world rolled and swayed, my blood sloshing like a tide with the rocking of the carriage. I listened to the sounds of the carriage rattling, the steady drum of hooves, the creak of the wheels beneath us. I was faintly aware of low voices.

"My God, Xenia. Such a rash tongue."

"I could not help myself. To think how she must suffer."

"It's bad, I'm sure. Still, I'm not inclined to suffer for her in exile. We'd make poor martyrs, you and I. At least I should."

"Forgive me." Her voice broke. "I want only to please you, and I am such a disappointment."

"No, no. Not ever." Andrei's voice gentled. "You are as close to heaven as I am likely to get."

"How could you not be disappointed?" she insisted. "I'm empty."

"It will come. Give it time."

She wept in soft, ragged breaths. "I pray. I search my heart. Why cannot I . . ."

"Darling." His voice thickened. "Hush." There was a long silence—just breathing—and a rustle of silk like dry leaves.

"She will wake," Xenia whispered.

He hushed her again. Something brushed against me. I opened my eyes but saw nothing. And then the moon sailed out from the clouds and silvered the velvety darkness into forms: one white breast, freed from Xenia's bodice and Andrei's profile poised over it. His head closed over her, and he began to suckle like an infant. Xenia's eyes were closed, her pink mouth slack, and I thought she might be asleep, except that she whimpered softly and sucked in her breath. Or perhaps this was me, for Andrei lifted his head. I clamped my eyes shut, shame flushing through me. When next I dared to steal a look, he had receded back into the dark. Xenia's breast was tucked back into its corset, but her fingers stretched out blindly, catching air, opening and closing like a sea flower. She sighed, lolled to her side, and curled into herself. Andrei began to hum some air I did not know. *If you look on me fair,* he warbled, *I shall not fear to die. And I shall not want more Heaven than what is in your eye.* The notes lingered lazily between the throb of blood in my ears. *This poor sinner only prays to be kissed to Paradise.*

Perhaps she knew I had heard them. The next morning, she told me that she had been to a priest some weeks earlier. As she spoke, she held one hand in the other and absently dug a thumbnail into the soft flesh of her palm.

"I begged him to pray for me, to cure me of my barrenness."

A practical man, the priest had first asked her whether she had sat on the ground as a child, for the cold might have made her infertile. No? That was good, he said. And did she ever lie with her husband on Saturdays or holy days? Xenia had replied that they refrained when it was right to do so. Well then, the priest pursued, when they did succumb, did she take pleasure from it?

"I had to confess that I could not help myself." She studied her palm and made another mark.

Here the priest found his answer: this barrenness was God's punishment for her lust. The act of fornication was evil, even between husband and wife. The only justification for this act was the children that came from it; without them, the soul remained stained. The cure was to repent of her sin and in future to avoid tempting her husband to his own damnation.

In desperation, she had proposed to Andrei that they should keep separate beds. But he could not be made to share her remorse and had laughed at the priest's suggestion. If they kept themselves chaste, how might they get children?

"I am so weak, Dasha." She looked confusedly at her hands, and her eyes filled. "Even at my soul's peril, I cannot bring myself to stop."

It may be that God looks with forbearance on such sinners. Night sounds from behind her door announced her continued failures, but within a few months of our conversation, I noticed that she had tied an acorn to the delicate cross and chain at her throat. Our peasant women wear them to assure an easy confinement. She did not speak of her expectation directly, though, for fear of bringing ill luck, nor would she suffer anyone else to. When she told her servant Marfa that her bodices should need to be let out, she answered the old woman's happy tears with childish insistence that she was only growing large on sweets; when she was sick to her stomach one morning and Marfa tried to soothe her by saying that this predicted a boy, Xenia spit thrice over her shoulder and ordered Marfa from the room.

Its presence swelled nonetheless, and though she forbade acknowledging the child, Xenia could not keep her hands from straying to her belly. Out of doors, she rested them there as though to shield the child from strangers. If her back or her feet ached, she would smile tiredly and say that it must be gout giving her trouble. She was more changeable than even she had been before, by turns gay and apprehensive. Then one day her labor was upon her.

A bed was prepared on the floor of her room and the midwife sent for. When this gaunt old woman arrived with her daughter, a copy of the mother but for a strawberry across her cheek, she sent everyone else from the room. For long hours, we waited in the passage, and so that her labor might be easier we pretended not to hear the moans coming from behind the closed door. She called out for Andrei, but he had gone downstairs because he could not bear anymore to hear her pain. Just after midnight, the midwife's daughter came out and handed me a packet of herbs.

"Boil this in water, and bring it back in the pot."

"Is she dying?" The sounds had become so terrible that it seemed no one could live through such agony.

The woman nodded to the herbs. "The willow and figwort will help her. Go on."

When I finally returned with the brew—how long should it boil, I wondered, and in how much water? One frets such things to tatters when the real worry cannot be addressed—I had time enough to glimpse Xenia through the opened door, wretched, white, and slick with sweat.

A few hours later, the daughter emerged again to report that Xenia had delivered a girl and both were well.

"May I see her?" I asked.

"She wants the father."

I went to fetch Andrei and told him that he had a daughter. He looked at me and said nothing, and I thought he might be disappointed by the news of a girl. But he was only slow to understand from having drunk too much. "A daughter, did you say?" He rushed up the stairs and did not emerge again for an hour. When he came out holding a little coffin—it was the afterbirth, to be buried under the house for good luck—he was as happy as I have ever seen a person.

It is custom to wash the newborn with cold water or roll it in the snow to harden it, but Xenia would not give up her child for this, no matter that the midwife contended that this would protect it from weakness and diseases. When the woman attempted to take charge of the matter forcibly, Xenia pushed her away and ordered her out of the house.

Xenia was like a she-bear with its cub, her affection was so fierce. She could not tolerate the briefest separation from the baby, and though I had cleared my things from my room, the distance from her own room was too great; she had the cradle hung next to her bed so that she might hear if the infant whimpered. She would not even give it up to a wet nurse but insisted on feeding it herself. Her mother's horror at this did not dissuade her; to Aunt Galya's protest that she was still unclean, she said, "Why should God give me milk unless He meant it to feed my baby?"

After the baptism, when Xenia was permitted to re-turn to society, she did so with reluctance. While out, she marked the hours till she could return home again. Aunt Galya warned her that such unchecked love for a child was dangerous. "You should not give your whole heart to any-thing mortal, daughter." Xenia was too far gone to heed her mother's counsel, so Aunt Galya appealed to Andrei.

"If you indulge her in this," she warned, "you will ruin mother and child both."

However, Andrei was himself smitten with the child, and he could not be shamed into exercising his authority. He permitted Xenia to name the child Catherine, which served no purpose, being neither the child's saint nor the name of anyone else who might protect her, and was only a fancy prompted by the news that the Grand Duchess was also with child again. When Xenia wished to make me the godmother, he did not object to this either, though it would have been wiser to choose a person with influence. For the baptism, he bought a gold cross for the infant's neck and a smock edged in lace, and nearly every week, he returned home with some new gift: a glass pendant to hang over the cradle, a silk pillow for the baby's head. If the child fussed and Xenia could not calm it, he sang airs to it himself, even leaving his guests downstairs to do so.

Aunt Galya threw up her hands. "How may a child learn obedience if she rules the parents? The egg cannot teach the hen." There was nothing more for her to do than leave this topsy-turvy household and return to Nadya's.

Xenia did indeed seem under the spell of her child. She would unswaddle the baby many times a day only to stare, fascinated, at the perfection of its tiny limbs. It was pretty, no harm can come from saying it now, though none of us would breathe it aloud at the time. She would giggle and say, "Is she not the ugliest creature you have ever seen?" and then she would kiss its toes and round belly and press her nose into its skin to inhale its yeasty smell.

Babies die, it is a sad but common fact of life.

There are mysteries that cannot be reasoned. Hail falls out of a clear sky and crushes the ripening field to rubble in an instant. The peasant who looks on and sees his broken stalks and blackened field may have lived well and piously or not, it does not change that his family will starve. And just so, a woman wakes one morning and finds her beloved daughter glazed with fever. The child shrieks and cannot be soothed. She twists away from the breast, her brow is hot as a stove, and even Saint-John's-wort and Epiphany water will not cool it. The doctor is called but can do nothing. And though the woman prays desperately and unceasingly, the child's cries shred the air for hours on end until, the only thing worse than these cries, they weaken and stop. By next morning, the child has grown too languid even to move her limbs, and there is only the rise and fall of her ribs, soft and rapid as a trapped bird. The hours eclipse, day to night to day again, before the tiny flame gutters and goes out.

Though we may try to tilt the universe with prayers and spells, medicines and every precaution, in the end the rain falls equally on the just and the unjust. What can be done but to face this mystery squarely and go on?

But Xenia could not accept it. "The air hurts." She said it with a wide-eyed wonder at her own pain. She suffered agonies of self-reproach, blaming herself for every sin her mother had cautioned her against—obstinacy and indulgence and putting another before God—and others that no one would have thought to reprove her for. If only she had done this or refrained from that: she continually uncovered fresh faults.

"When I think how I have lived . . ." She said this to Nadya, choking on her tears and then going on with rigid determination. "When I recall that I have spent whole days pondering whether to have a gown styled in the French or the Spanish fashion, how my hair should be arranged, whether to put a beauty mark on my cheek or on my shoulder, as though any of it mattered! As though it were not all foolishness and frippery!"

Nadya was offended. "You might think that no one had ever lost a child before you. This was not even a son."

Xenia scourged herself further, saying that Nadya was right, her grief showed a lack of humility before God's will. She wept bitterly and long at this.

Five days after the death of Xenia's child, the Imperial family was at last given an heir, the Grand Duke Paul. Overjoyed, the Empress whisked the new infant from his mother's arms and installed him in a room adjacent to her own that she might look after him personally. Or so it was reported. The Grand Duchess, having acquitted herself of her duty, was left untended in her birthing bed for days. It was from this bed that she received report that Elizabeth had sent her lover, Saltykov, off to Sweden to announce the birth to the king. When he returned in the new year, he would be sent away again.

Petersburg drowned in celebration. Such giddy exultation—every night a supper, a ball, a concert, and more than the usual number of drinking parties. Hymns

were composed to glorify the infant, and Andrei was con-
tinuously called upon to perform the celebratory offices of
the choir, though these did not fully account for his many
long absences.

There was talk, of course—half the English Embank-
ment had been woken by loud and ribald singing, and the
next morning Andrei had arrived late to the Empress's chapel, wobbly-legged and with stains on his waistcoat—but
Xenia did not hear the talk, for she could no longer tolerate
society. The prospect of enduring endless, nattering gossip,
of having to dance and pretend to gaiety . . . she could not
do it. Invited by Madame Polianskaya to yet another supper
honoring the royal birth, she told Andrei that she would
rather the skin were flayed from her flesh. He was left to
devise a more suitable explanation for her absence.

The face Andrei kept turned to the world remained
merry, but inside his own door he swung at times to the
other extreme and became morose, as though mirth had
exhausted him. But whether gay or sad, he drank as though
feeding a fire, and his mood would burn itself out only after
hours or even days of intensity.

Xenia had never seen her husband's excesses as faults.
She had once explained it to me thus: an unrestrained nature came with his gift. It was what made him sensitive to
every note of music, why his voice could move others to
tears. Araja or Teplov might pen the notes, but Xenia saw
their scores as merely a poor representation, as far from the
music itself as a drawing of a horse is from animate flesh
and breath.

"They're only scratches on a page," she said. "But when he sings, one feels the presence of God in the air. It reverberates in the bones. Truly, it shatters me, it is so real." Andrei was an open conduit through which this terrible power surged; how could he be other than passionate?

Now, though, she was too far sunk in her own misery to recognize the form his grief took. Nightly, we sat up awaiting his return and listening to the crackle and boom of fireworks that convulsed the sky over the city. When he finally came home, so dissipated that he could not keep his feet, she brought him his kvas, warmed with honey and herbs for his throat, and then sat in silence, watching him drink.

"Go to bed," he implored us. I bid him good night and waited for Xenia on the stair, but she did not follow.

"I cannot sleep," she said to him. "My heart is too loud. It keeps beating and beating, like an imprisoned creature pounding to get out. I beg God to still it, but He will not."

"You might yet have another child, even many more."

It was said with gentleness, but she was stricken. "I have lost my happiness. Do you think I may simply forget our Katenka? I don't have your capacity." She hid her face in her hands and did not see what I saw: the surprise of hurt in his eyes, the way his jaw slowly worked at this bile before swallowing it. Afterwards, he often stayed away past dawn and even for days at a time.

The air in Petersburg was thick with talk of the infant Grand Duke. We refrained from any mention of it in Xenia's presence, but the world is full of babies, including one under her own roof that belonged to the servant Masha.

This child's crib hung from a rafter in the corner of the kitchen, close to the hearth and out of the way. It lay there most hours unnoticed, sucking on its *soska*, the little cloth bag of gruel that kept it mostly quiet. But Xenia was so susceptible to this child's presence that if it did cry, wherever she might be in the house she heard it. Her mouth and eyes would tighten as though she were being tortured, as though the Secret Chancery were pulling out her fingernails one by one. If no one happened to be in the kitchen to still the child, Xenia was compelled to go to it; she could not help herself. I sometimes found her at the crib, clutching the baby to her breast and soothing it. But more often, her own face mirrored the tearful infant's, and then she would rebuke Masha for allowing the child to be soiled or hungry. Masha was not neglectful, or no more so than any mother whose labors are divided, but because Xenia was so sensitive, the whole household tried to keep the child from her notice as much as was possible.

Of all Xenia's former pleasures, only hymns that were sung in the church still soothed her. You might not think it to see her—she would listen with water coursing down her cheeks—but no, she said, the music was a relief. "I do not think." Sometimes at home she hummed a line of the litany, repeating the same phrase over and over. If I happened upon her then, she would startle, bewildered, as though she had wakened in a strange place, and then her countenance would assume its remembered sorrow.

## CHAPTER SIX

Four months after the death of the child and a week before Christmas, Xenia sent for me where I was dining at Kuzma Zakharovich's. Aunt Galya had arranged it in order that I should meet a certain gentleman there, an acquaintance of Kuzma Zakharovich visiting from Moscow. I knew nothing else of him except that he was unmarried and in need of a wife. I suspect Aunt Galya had only surmised the latter, for when we were introduced, it was evident he knew nothing of me either and was surprised to have me sprung upon him, as it were.

We had not yet sat down to supper when Xenia's houseboy, Grishka, came with a message saying that his mistress required me urgently. I immediately made my apologies and departed.

When I arrived at the house, I saw Xenia's figure through the open doorway of the drawing room. "I've come as quickly as . . ." The words dried on my tongue when she turned and I saw it was Andrei. He was wearing an apricot-colored damask gown of Xenia's that had been let out and refashioned for him, but not skillfully. His broad chest strained against the bodice, and incongruous tufts of dark hair curled over the top. Balancing on his head was a lady's powdered wig.

My surprise and discomfort were reflected in his own face. "It's another of her wretched fancies." He waved a naked forearm—like a mutton shank edged in white lace—in the general direction of the Winter Palace.

The Imperial ball that evening was to be a metamorphoses, the men compelled to dress as women and the women to don breeches and jackets.

Our sovereign, he mused, was partial to these evenings because she had once looked so well in men's clothes, with her fine legs shown off to advantage. "No doubt, her pleasure is increased by how ludicrous everyone else looks." He swayed across the room, swatting at his skirt with annoyance. "Have you come to gawk at me?"

I didn't know where to rest my eyes. "Is Xenia ill?"

"No, cousin, not ill." He picked up a wineglass sitting beside an empty decanter. The glass was all but empty as well, but he lifted it to his lips anyway and, tilting back his head, caused his towering wig to list dangerously. He caught at it and grimaced, as though the victim of a prank.

"She slept poorly and has been in a state all day, insisting that we mustn't go to the palace tonight."

He readjusted the wig, trying without success to prop it in such a way that he might rescue the last drops from the bottom of his glass. "God knows, I would happily oblige her if I could, but we have been particularly invited."

Empress Elizabeth's constant entertainments, once a source of delight, had become a tedious obligation and a formidable expense. By Imperial edict, dresses might be worn at court only just the once, and to enforce this, pages were set at the door to dab ink on the skirts of departing guests.

Still, those favored with an invitation to the Winter Palace balls were compelled to attend, and Andrei worried that Xenia's absence might be reported. The recent poor health of Her Imperial Majesty had made her intolerant of others' excuses. Last month, she had sent cadets to Alexi Arkharov's home to see if he was indeed ill. When he was discovered with nothing more than a slight cough, she had ordered him dragged out into a snowbank and left there until he was adequately sick.

"Perhaps my wife will listen to you," Andrei said. "I cannot bend her."

"I shall try."

"And if you would indulge me further, tell Ivan to fetch up another bottle."

I found Xenia in bed, sunk against a raft of pillows. Since little Katenka's death, she had lost all color in her face and her eyes had become dull, but tonight they held a glitter like fever.

"He must think I do not love him. I promised obedience, and now when he asks it . . . I thought I would give up my life for him, but it seems I cannot."

I put my hand to her forehead. "In heaven's name, what are you talking about?"

She grasped my hand to still it. "I dreamt my own death." Her eyes were far away. "I was falling. I was tumbling down the front steps of the palace, but I could see it happening, as though I were watching from a high window. Someone screamed, and then I was lying on the snow at the bottom of the steps." She gazed at the far wall as though a drama were playing out before her, and she narrating as it unfolded. "A darkness bloomed round my head. At first I thought it was a shadow thrown on the snow by torches." Her voice broke, and she fell silent for a moment before resuming. "There was a confusion of voices, but I remember someone said to send for a priest. Another person argued no, a priest might arouse the suspicions of Her Imperial Majesty. 'If she asks,' this person said, 'you must say only that a guest has fallen. You know how she abhors any mention of death.' That is how I knew."

"Xenia—" I began.

"I felt such agony, and when I woke, I knew it was a warning from God."

What answer could I make to this?

Xenia, though, had devised a plan. I should go in her place. It was a metamorphosis, after all. If I wore her costume, kept to myself, and said nothing, no one might discover the ruse.

An outlandish scheme, perhaps—only in plays are such swapped identities believed—yet saying no to Xenia was more unthinkable to me than her plot. Perhaps it was not such a leap as I imagined. After all, who knew her better than I? I allowed myself to be persuaded.

Her costume had been laid out over a chair: one of Andrei's uniforms, a pair of stockings, and small buckled shoes
in a man's style. The jacket and breeches were too long for
my person, but this did not dissuade Xenia.

"Grishka is of your proportions." She sent for him, and
when he appeared asked him to relinquish his new livery.
The poor boy misunderstood and was distraught at what he
might have done to provoke the loss of his position. Xenia
explained that I was merely borrowing his garments for the
evening, which did nothing to relieve his confusion. "Go
on"—she motioned for his baize jacket, which he abashedly
removed. She waited for the rest, but then relented. "See
that your breeches are sent back up straightaway."

"We can tack some lace at the sleeves and neck," she said
to me.

Once we had bound my breasts, the jacket fitted me, as
did the rest of the livery. With my hair pulled back into a
tail, I resembled to the passing eye a boy in service. But I
bore no likeness to Xenia.

"Nor would I resemble myself if I were costumed. That's
the entire point of the metamorphosis."

Had he been sober, who knows if Andrei would have
allowed this charade to go forward. As it was, when we
came downstairs he was far enough into his wine to have
abandoned discretion. He gaped at me, making me pain-
fully conscious of my legs, their shape exposed in the tight
cloth of the breeches.

"What is this? Are you coming to the ball as our footman?"

Xenia revealed her plan, and Andrei laughed. "So I am to go as you, Xenia? And Dasha is also to go as you? If only you will come as yourself, we might be a holy trinity."

She looked miserable.

"It's madness." He chuckled. "No one will be deceived."

"I'm so sorry."

"Nonsense, I'm not complaining. One wife at home, another at court—were I not wearing a skirt, I should be feeling quite vigorous right now."

FROM A LONG WAY OFF, I could see the Winter Palace, its windows lit like a row of polished gold ingots. As we neared, I felt fresh stirrings of apprehension; when we passed through the gates and I saw the line of sleighs disgorging their occupants, my apprehension spilt over.

Grishka waited, his hand held out, his eyes trained fixedly on nothing, his features rigid with the effort to disregard his own livery and the ridiculous picture we made: one footman helping another to alight. He then offered his hand to Andrei, who was obliged to accept it in order that he might manage his skirts. Snatching his fan back from Grishka, Andrei took my arm in his free hand only to drop it again so that he might lift his hem as we mounted the steps and then marble staircase inside. I had no need of his hand anyway; being costumed as a man, I could move unencumbered. Not a thing prevented my taking the steps two at a time, save my dread of arriving at the top.

On the landing, an Imperial page received our invitation and announced us. My knees turned liquid. I had no skirt to hide their quaking, no fan to hide the rising color in my face. Andrei whispered in my ear, "Don't look so stricken. Pretend an interest in who else is here."

At a glance, the scene appeared the twin of other Imperial balls: hundreds of lavishly costumed persons so crowded into the room that their skirts touched, color to color, like a jumble of mosaic tiles. If only I could step back, I thought, the confusion might resolve into a design. My desire to withdraw was made all the more powerful by the airless stench in the room. I felt faint and patted my pockets for Xenia's little enameled box of herbs. I distinctly remembered tucking it in my jacket. But no, that had been the other jacket, the one of Andrei's that had been too large. Andrei grasped an elbow to still my skittering hands.

He guided me into the room. "Don't let yourself be engaged in conversation."

"What if someone should address me?"

"Smile or be aloof, depending on the person. But keep quiet."

Although the scene was familiar from other such gatherings, there was an ineffable difference, a slight distortion as if reflected in a poor mirror. The ladies appeared taller and bulkier than their male partners, who, for their part, seemed to have shrunk like old men, their shoulders and calves thin as sticks. As we neared, this dissonance grew, persons changing sexes or wavering uncertainly between one sex and the other.

A stout merchant's wife rumbled in a basso profundo

about the difficulty of keeping her troops supplied. "I have been six weeks now awaiting a signature."

Her companion, a swarthy woman in yellow brocade, nodded glumly. "It's true. She schools us, her children, in the virtue of patience." The woman absently plucked feathers from a fan clutched in her thick-knuckled hand. "My wife has borne two children while I await some word on Prussia." Before my eyes, her face sprouted stubble and she assumed the appearance of a poorly camouflaged man. All about us, such transformations unfolded as we moved into the room. It was unsettling.

Andrei scanned the room like a hound searching the scent. At last he found it in the person of a very long-limbed woman standing near a window at the far end of the room. She stood apart, not only by virtue of being alone but also because she stood a full head taller than anyone in the room. Further, she alone had disregarded the injunction to wear breeches and was costumed instead in a hoop-less white gown that skimmed her form. I guessed by the crown of olive leaves in her hair that she was meant to be one of the Roman goddesses.

Andrei approached and addressed her in Italian. Her fan swished open in greeting, and she loosed a trill of words. Like birdsong, it was exquisite to hear. Andrei's low and labored Italian alternated like a duet with her lilting voice. Though I could not translate their words, the matter revealed itself in their expressions and gestures. Andrei was flattering her. It looks the same in any language. With an expansive gesture, he praised her appearance. She held her pose but indicated modesty by the transfer of her gaze downwards. He repeated himself in more insistent tones; again, she demurred by tilting her chin and showing her profile, but I saw she was pleased.

She bore a startling resemblance to the cranes we sometimes saw, posed and motionless, in the marshes near our country house. Her arms were exceedingly long and seemed too delicate to support even the weight of a fan. Her head, dominated by a beakish nose, balanced precariously on a reed-like neck. She had small, dark eyes. Another woman of just her proportions might have been thought ugly. But she carried herself with such elegance, each gesture arrived at and held with such attention, that like the crane's, her awkwardness was made graceful. Once I had formed this idea of her, her white breast seemed the counterfeit of the bird's and the lace half-concealing it resembled feathers. I fairly expected her to spear up a fish at any moment.

Directing her fan at me, she warbled a question.

*"La mia moglie,"* Andrei answered. "Xenia Grigoryevna." He turned to me. "Xenia, may I present Signor Francesco Gaspari."

I was shocked, and not solely to discover that he was a man. You see, I knew the name. Who did not? It was lately on the lips of all Petersburg society, in loud praise for the purity of his singing and also in salacious whispers. He was what is called a musico. A sacred monster. A eunuch.

Lifting my hand, he kissed it a moment longer than was fashionable. *"Sono incantanto,"* he said, followed by a ripple of syllables beyond my understanding. I felt myself coloring

and was relieved when Andrei coaxed his attention outwards. He asked the musico some question, and the two
began to speak in lowered tones, though Gaspari's voice
still tinkled an octave higher than Andrei's.

"*La Principessa di Courland,*" Gaspari whispered, and
raised his eyebrows meaningfully. "*Sta conversando con
l'ambasciatore olandese. E quella è la sorella del Signor Shuvalov.*"

In past seasons, the cognoscenti had reserved all their
raptures for another musico, Lorenzo Saletti. No one, they
had said, could equal his Berenice. One might have thought
that his being of middle years, wrinkled, and shaped like a
dumpling would have marred his impersonation of a young
maiden, but not so; for the aficionado, it was the voice
alone that mattered, and there was even said to be a particular thrill in such confusion of the senses. However, when
Saletti left the employ of the Imperial court and returned
to Italy to recover his health, allegiances had shifted with
alacrity. In Araja's most recent opera, the famed Giovanni
Carestini had sung the *primo uomo* role, and in place of the
departed Saletti, this Gaspari had taken the secondary part.
These two had dazzled Petersburg with their bravura. They
were said to be like a pair of preening peacocks, unfurling
glorious trills and flourishes, one displaying and then the
other answering with mounting virtuosity until women
fainted from their chairs. Such sweet tones were too divine,
the cognoscenti crooned, to come from mortal men.

Even up close, there was no telltale sign of manhood, no
shadow of a beard, no Adam's apple. Gaspari's wrists were
slender as a lady's, and his figure had the soft and rounded

shapes no man can feign. Yet he was not quite female, either. He had the appearance of having been put together from the parts of different persons. I cannot explain how this worked on me except to admit that I could not easily wrest my eyes from him. He was at once repugnant and fascinating.

I could pick out only the occasional name from the stream of their conversation, but I followed their eyes and the movements of Gaspari's fan. Like a weather vane in a shifting breeze, it wavered and held in one direction and then in another as he pointed out various persons in the room. Their disguises were no hindrance to him; he seemed to know the identity of everyone. Perhaps it was for this reason that Andrei had sought him out.

Gaspari's fan singled out a thin-faced woman in the lacy garb of a dandy and identified her as Countess Stroganova. Her name, I recalled, had been linked to his. If the rumors that circulated round him were to be believed, his being unmanned was no impediment to his skills as a lover. He was as famous for his love affairs as for his voice, and it was said that certain practical ladies in the court preferred him over men who might get them with child. Others whispered that, though he was himself without sensation, he could pleasure a woman until she was nearly dead of it.

My glance stole from the Countess back to Gaspari, and I found him looking at me knowingly. "We are not . . ." he began, and then halted. Tapping his temple with his fan, he asked Andrei, *"Che cos'è la vostra parola per 'sembra'?"*

"Appear."

He turned back and ducked his long neck towards me to whisper, "We are not what we appear, *signora*. Yes?"

It was the sort of banal observation that persons say when they are in costume and cannot think of an original remark, but I heard more in it, as though he were confiding something to a fellow conspirator.

The musicians lumbered into a solemn polonaise and every eye turned, anticipating the arrival of Her Imperial Majesty. It was not she, however, but the Grand Duke and Duchess.

Had one but the wit to see it, the future was writ large in their appearances. Everything that made Peter seem unfit to rule was magnified by his being in feminine attire. He looked feeble and foolish, a sickly girl with narrow shoulders and lanky, thin arms. It did not go unremarked, moreover, that his gown was made of Prussian blue, like a thumb in the eye of his people. By contrast, Grand Duchess Catherine had elected to dress in the uniform of the Preobrazhensky Guards, her thick chestnut hair tied with a simple ribbon beneath the hat. She was splendid and strong and carried herself with such uncompromising dignity that she might have been born to wear breeches.

As they processed into the hall, Peter mechanically offered his arm to his wife. She took it without seeming to notice his presence. The assembled courtiers fell into line to be received, and, as the royal couple passed, Catherine obligingly acknowledged her guests. Peter glowered at them, as though he were looking over his subjects for one he might whip. The courtiers fell in behind them, processing into the polonaise.

As they approached our threesome, I dropped into a deep curtsy, noting as I did that without the cover of skirts, my knees splayed unattractively. I raised my eyes in time to see His Imperial Highness salute the musico with an excessive, smirking courtesy. His eyes darted maliciously to gauge his wife's reaction, but she was resolutely impassive.

*"Mi permetta?"* Gaspari proffered his arm to me, the fingers extended daintily. "You would do me the honor?"

Having been cautioned by Andrei against speaking, I looked to him now for rescue, but he offered no assistance and, stepping back, gallantly handed me off to the musico.

It was part of the Empress's enforced amusement that the women should lead their partners. However, a lady up the line was so tentative in this that dancers had begun to pile up behind her, and the men, unaccustomed to the girth of their skirts, threatened to topple the whole pattern like dominoes. Like a troupe of clowns, we made our graceless promenade round the hall until at long last it was cleared of nearly all but the Imperial servants stationed at arm's length along each wall. A hundred or more of them in their green-and-yellow livery stood at attention, giving the impression of guards placed to prevent any disheartened guest from escaping the dance. I searched in vain for an apricot dress.

"It seems Andrei Feodorovich he has left you in my care." Gaspari had read my look. "Perhaps he has been discovered by a friend of his wife?" His dark eyes were mischievous.

I felt myself flush.

"I have seen Xenia Grigoryevna." He reached for my hand and feathered the back of it with his fingers. "She is more white and more tall."

He smiled and did not let go of my hand. "You do this why?" Tipping his head to one side, he waited on me to answer. For all that it was a pose, his curiosity was not unkind.

"She is my friend and she was . . . she needed me."

He nodded approvingly. "That is a good answer. I would like such a friend." He lifted my hand to his painted lips. "If you are not too *fatiguée* . . . ?" The line of dancers had begun to divide into two parallel columns, threatening to strand us between them. "The bird may hide best in the . . ." He searched for a word. "Many?" He fluttered his fingers.

"The flock," I said.

"*Sì, sì*, the flock, *sì*." He gestured me towards the line of mock men and fell back with the other mock women.

Through this gauntlet, each couple was compelled to come together and process at a pace measured enough to allow the onlookers' appraisal. The polonaise is the most stately of dances, designed to display the nobility of the dancer. But garbed as they were, an attitude of nobility was beyond the reach of most. The women took pains to rise above their discomfort; robbed of their wigs and their fans and with their fat or spindly calves on exhibit, they nevertheless cast proud looks down the line, as though to hold themselves aloof from their own ridiculousness. But few of the men troubled to disguise their ill-humor at being exposed to mockery; they resembled humiliated prisoners being led to the gallows. The glittering lights of the candelabra could not dispel the heavy air in the room.

Only Gaspari seemed not to feel it. Perhaps he had long ago accustomed himself to mortification, but standing across from me, he looked enviably at his ease, an elegant and haughty woman among graceless sisters. Such was the confusion worked on me by the metamorphoses that I found myself grateful to be partnered with him, and not only because he seemed disinclined to expose my secret. When he stepped lightly to my side and we moved arm in arm into the maw, I was emboldened by feeling invisible beside him.

The columns blended and divided again, and now first the gentlemen and then the ladies passed through the gauntlet unaccompanied. As I felt each person fall away ahead of me, my dread returned and deepened. My turn came. The line opened and then closed up again behind me, and I processed with painful slowness, like a mouse through the guts of a snake. *Step, step, chassé.* I repeated it silently. The tunnel of faces down which I moved was interminable, a thousand eyes staring as though to burn away my costume and expose me. I felt particularly conscious of my hands and could not recall what to do with them. *Step, step, chassé. Step, step, chassé.* At last I reached the end and gasped up air like a dying fish. Gaspari gave me a solicitous look from across the gap before the shifting dancers reeled him away, and with new partners the figure was repeated.

The figures of the polonaise are endless. At some point, I thought I saw Andrei or at least a part of him. He was standing in the company of two others, who hid him from view, but the back of his apricot gown was reflected in the dark gleam of a window. When next I was returned to that vantage point, he was gone.

The dancers began to move sullenly together and apart like the mechanical figures of a clock, excepting when the mathematics of the dance coupled two who were already linked by gossip. When the Grand Duchess Catherine linked arms with Count Stanislav Poniatowsky, the British ambassador's secretary, their approach was heralded by an airy rush of whispers, like a wave rippling down the length of a pebbled shore. I had become numb to the torment of passing through the line and had fallen to contemplating smaller mortifications—the weariness of my feet within their buckled shoes, the chafing of my bound breasts— when the lady on my left caught sight of a promising diversion and alerted the gentleman facing her.

*"Attendez."* She nodded in the direction of an approaching couple. "You know," she whispered, "she carried on with that creature for months, and right under the Count's nose. Naturally, he never suspected. It was only her dog that betrayed her."

Our two lines parted for the couple to pass, and the Countess Stroganova sailed into view, her hand resting at the slender waist of Gaspari.

My mind struggled to reconcile the picture. They looked too much alike to be lovers. With their fingers touching lightly tip to tip, he might have been her image reversed and elongated by the distortion of a poor mirror. I wondered how it would be to lie with someone who was in all ways but one a sister.

"What of the dog?" the gentleman asked. We had come together again with the requisite bows and curtseys.

"When the monster came to their house to sing, her little spaniel ran up to it and licked at its ankles like an old friend. Thus she was exposed."

At last we were returned to our original partners and rewarded with the promise of supper. The guests waited to enter the adjacent hall in order of precedence, and from this clutch Andrei appeared, looking a bit untidy but merry.

"Xenia, my dear wife!" Each of his exhalations announced how he had spent the past hours. "I thought I had lost you." He grasped both my hands as though we had been parted for months and, turning, thanked Gaspari effusively for keeping me amused. "I'm grieved to have missed seeing the promenade. A Frenchman would not let me go. You two must promise to dance a minuet after supper so I may have a second chance."

A page approached Gaspari to direct him to his seat. He took my hand and lifted it to his painted lips. *"Arrivederci per ora."*

When he was out of earshot, I whispered, "Signor Gaspari knows I am not Xenia."

Andrei waved off the news breezily. "It's no matter. He's the soul of indiscretion, but there are few here who would deign to hear anything from him but music."

"Is he to sing?"

"No, he claims the Grand Duke invited him personally. My guess is that it's His Imperial Highness's notion of a jest, seating him above the salt like that, a bit of scandal to irk the Grand Duchess."

Our own seats placed us across from the counterfeits of a young sailor and an older Cossack. Andrei greeted the Cossack, who looked at him questioningly. "It is Colonel Petrov." Andrei swooped into a low bow, forgetting his wig. He snatched at it, righted the nest atop his head, and smiled ingratiatingly.

"I am grateful you do not know me in this hideous getup. But no costume can disguise your beauty, Madame Lopukhina. May I present my wife, Xenia Grigoryevna. I hope you will forgive her; the cold weather has made her hoarse."

It was Andrei's habit to be pleasing, and drink only made him more courtly. With each course, he grew more lively and expansive.

At three o'clock, the throne was still conspicuously empty. As no one might leave before Her Imperial Majesty arrived, the assembled guests rose from supper and plodded round the dance floor again like beaten nags. Endless refrains of a minuet issued from the nodding musicians and kept the dancers at their paces.

At last Her Imperial Majesty arrived. Whatever relief might have been felt was snuffed by her appearance. She entered the hall with uncharacteristic slowness and leaned heavily on the arm of Ivan Ivanovich Shuvalov, her legs too swollen to bear her full weight.

I have sometimes consoled myself that having been born without beauty, I have not suffered the loss of it. Those who take delight in their own physiognomy and who see themselves reflected in the admiring eyes of the world must feel each wrinkle as keenly as the cut of a razor. At the peak of her bloom, Elizabeth Petrovna's beauty had been inspiration for the poets and painters of the age and had known no rivals. What rivals appeared later she had quashed, forbidding them to wear pink in her presence or to adorn themselves with jewels that might outshine her own. She had surrounded herself with flatterers and had taken as favorites a string of boys in whose company she might feel her own youth again. Only a monarch may be so self-deceiving, but no amount of fawning could conceal the truth any longer. She was old and sick, and one could see in her eyes the desperate rage of a trapped animal.

Even at her best, Her Imperial Majesty was notoriously hard to please, and the courtiers were in no mood to make the attempt now. As they fell into line to be received by their sovereign and fulfill their duty, they discreetly signaled pages to have their horses readied. The moment the Empress had lumbered past us, Andrei guided me into the throng flowing towards the door.

We emerged into the late December night. The sharp air cut through my cloak and stung my legs but revived me like a tonic. I admired the glittering sky and the lights of the palace falling across the snow in gold stripes. A buzz swelled at our backs as more and more guests emerged from the hive.

Andrei was merry. He snatched off his wig and, tossing it onto the step, stamped on it as if killing a rat.

"What a night! But we survived our test. To think of you dancing with Gaspari!" He laughed. "I am as lucky as a sultan in my wives." He swooped in and woozily swiped my cheek with his lips, and began to sing the same light ditty I had first overheard in the carriage years before and that so often came unthinking to his lips. *If you look on me fair, my love, I shall not fear to die. And I shall not want more Heaven than what is in your eye.* The familiar notes thawed the frozen air. *This poor sinner only prays to be kissed to Paradise.*

Our sleigh moved to the head of the line, and Grishka leapt down. Andrei said something, but the wind off the river whipped it away. Smiling, he took a step up towards me, and reached out his hand. Suddenly, it was snatched away. The bell of his skirt flew up, and he disappeared behind an explosion of white underskirts and dark limbs.

It was over in an instant. In retrospect, I can only guess that he caught a heel in the wig and, being drunk, could not recover his balance. In a blink, he was sprawled motionless in front of the sleigh, the rigid hoop of his skirt obscuring his face from me. I ran down the stone steps to where he lay. He seemed to be looking up at me. Round his head, a red flower bloomed in the snow.

I sank to the ground and, lifting his head, rested it in my lap. It was heavy as iron. The bee buzz of the crowd seemed far away and had a quality like silence. I waited. Faces wavered into view and then faded back into darkness.

No priest or doctor came. I grew first cold and then numb. After an indeterminate length of time, Ivan and Grishka lifted Andrei's body and carried it away.

"*Signorina?*" A light hand rested on my shoulder. "You must go to your friend. I will take you, if you please."

## CHAPTER SEVEN

I returned to Andrei's house in the company of Gaspari, with Andrei's sleigh bearing his body behind us.

When I entered the drawing room, Xenia was curled on the divan under a lap blanket. She sat up and looked at me drowsily. On the point of making some remark, she suddenly blanched, her eyes fixed at my waist. Looking down, I saw my tunic and breeches were stained with blood.

"There was an accident," I began, but my throat closed.

She sprang up and ran past Gaspari, out into the dark, where she was met with the sight of Ivan and Grishka bearing her husband's corpse from the sleigh.

Xenia howled. I have never heard such a terrible noise except from wolves. Then she threw herself at his body with such wildness that the alarmed servants laid him down where they were and withdrew. Bent over him, she keened, stroking his face and then shaking him as though to force him back to life.

I went to her and put my hand to her back. At my touch,

she wrenched herself round to face me: green fires pulsed in her eyes, violent and remote as the aurora lights. I was afraid.

By now, the whole of the house had been roused from their beds, and one by one they gathered at the door. Their grief chorused beneath hers.

I know not how long Xenia went on, but at last her strength gave out. Drawing her breath in hiccoughs and gasps, she slumped over the body and was too exhausted to resist when I lifted her off him. I gave orders that she be carried to her bed and that Andrei's body also be taken inside. A soft voice behind me said, "I have send my carriage for a priest." Turning, I saw the musico. I had forgotten he was there. Tears had etched runnels in his powdered and rouged cheeks. He looked ludicrous.

"I may do some further service?" he asked.

I thanked him and said that I could manage, but he seemed not to understand. He made no move to take his leave.

"Without the carriage, I have no means home, *signorina*. And I cannot danger the voice." He patted his throat. I noticed then that he was shivering with cold.

"Oh, forgive me. Come inside. We will wait for the priest together."

I have no further recollection of that morning. In the front hall, I sat down that my boots might be removed, and rested my head against the wall. As soon as I was off my feet, I was gone.

When I awoke, it was still dark. Or dark again, I did not

know. I smelt incense and heard the murmur of someone praying, and instantly remembered, though what I remembered had the quality of a dream. I stood up and moved like a somnambulist towards this low voice. In the drawing room, Andrei's body had been laid out on a table. A cloth had been spread over him to serve as a funeral pall and hide that he was still clothed in Xenia's dress. Two candlesticks were placed at his head, and their dim pool illuminated Andrei's features as well as the face of a priest bent close, reading the prayers. *As the waters fail from the sea, and the flood decayeth and drieth up, so man lieth down, and riseth not: till the heavens be no more, they shall not awake, nor be raised out of their sleep.* His voice was low and intimate, as though he were in private conversation with Andrei. *O that thou wouldest hide me in the grave, that thou wouldest keep me in secret till thy wrath be past.* I had the strange thought that I should not disturb them, but I stayed in the doorway for a time, letting the words crest over me.

Without benefit of a taper, I felt my way up the stairs and to Xenia's room. She was still clothed and propped upright on her bed, but she did not respond to my coming in. When I asked Masha if her mistress had slept, she said no, and then yes, and then that she did not know. She crossed herself and wept.

"Xenia?" I whispered. She did not answer. Her face was gray, and her eyes, though open, were entirely empty. I was put in mind first of Andrei lying downstairs and then of the wax effigy of Tsar Peter that resides in the Kunstkamera. Seated on a great throne, it glares so steadily that one is compelled to look away. Only upon nervous sidewise

glances can one detect the ruse: though it is in all other
ways the perfect copy of a man, the figure is too still and
the enamel eyes have no animation. Even so, it is too disquieting to contemplate directly.

So it was with Xenia. I took her limp hand into mine.
Her gaze, directed towards the stove, remained blank. I
noted the subtle rising and falling of her chest. "Should I
stoke the fire?" I asked, as though I were responding to a
subtle hint.

The room was already sufficiently warm, but not knowing what else to do, I sent Masha downstairs to fetch some
brandy, and busied myself with the tinderbox. I devoted
excessive attention to my task until Masha returned with
the brandy.

"Here, this will revive you." My voice in my own ears
sounded like pots clattering to the floor, but Xenia remained insensible. I held the glass up and pressed it against
her lips, but she did not drink. "Here, just a sip," I coaxed.
Tilting back her head, I poured the liquid into her opened
mouth. It dribbled back out and ran down her chin. "You
must try, darling." She made no answer.

"We should get her out of these clothes and into bed.
Sleep is the best thing." I removed her stockings and wrested
her loose of her bodice. Her inert limbs provided no assistance and were remarkably heavy in their inanimate state,
but with Masha's assistance I freed her of her petticoats. We
pulled a nightgown down over her head, worked her arms
into the sleeves, and then arranged her limbs in an attitude
of repose, with her gaze redirected at the ceiling.

I do not recall the feeble winter sun rising or setting, only perpetual darkness broken at intervals by my imperfect vigil. Like the apostles in Gethsemane, I tried to keep awake and pray but could not. So it went for an unmarked procession of time. The priest downstairs chanted the psalms over Andrei's body, mourners came and left, but I took no notice of them, nor of the servants, who, being so suddenly deprived of both master and mistress, left off their customary duties and gathered aimlessly in the halls and the yard.

At some point, I was called downstairs to see Nadya, who had appeared at the house complaining that she and her mother had not received mourning cards to inform them of Andrei's death and had learnt of it only as strangers might. "Our mother was offered condolences by a neighbor in the street," she fumed.

"Xenia is overcome with grief," I said.

"Do you know he is laid out in a woman's dress? With only a priest praying over him, and some strange woman? His friends shall think Xenia unfeeling. There is no coffin lid at the door, and the girl told me that no preparations have been made for the funeral dinner."

When I answered that these duties were quite beyond Xenia's capacity, that she could not even rise from her bed, Nadya went up the stairs, thinking, I suppose, to scold her sister into action. Finding her immune to rebuke did not soften Nadya's mood.

"Has she been bled?"

I replied that she had not.

"I shall send my surgeon." Shaking her head, she left.

Andrei was without family, excepting some distant cousins in Little Russia. As for Xenia's close relations, evidently Aunt Galya was too distraught by the news of her daughter being widowed to come to the house, and Nadya was too vexed to return. There being no more immediate candidates in line for the offices of family, I elected myself. With Masha, I first washed Andrei's body and dressed him in his uniform, then had a casket sent from the cabinet-maker. There is a tremendous amount to do when someone leaves the world. I ordered more flour and nuts and vodka, boiled wheat for the *kolivo*, and set Marfa in the kitchen to making blinis. Masha was charged with watching Xenia and changing her bedding while I gathered up her clothes for dyeing. When the surgeon came, I left off plucking a goose and escorted him upstairs.

The surgeon was a brisk man. He gave Xenia hardly a glance before unpacking his instruments and setting the cups onto the stove to warm. Pulling a chair to her bedside, he took her limp arm, pushed up its sleeve, and tied it off above the elbow with a strip of linen. He worked the arm like a pump and then studied its length, flicking his middle finger against the skin.

"She has been like this for near two days now," I said.

He nodded and took up the other arm. His self-possession was comforting. When he found a vein to his liking, he removed a lancet from its case, cocked the spring, and by means of a button released it, driving the blade into her flesh. Xenia jerked, blood bubbled up, and he covered the wound with one of the heated glass cups. The cup was shaped like a hand bell topped with a brass nipple. Into this he fastened a syringe. This further encouraged the vein to breathe by sucking out the blood and ill humors. When the cup was full, he instructed me to fetch a bleeding bowl from his box. He emptied the cup and put on another. At this, Xenia turned her dull, fish-eyed gaze upon her arm. The sight of her blood seemed to provoke a terror in her, for she started to shriek, to tremble all over, and to sputter unintelligible noises. The surgeon, far from being alarmed, expressed satisfaction at her liveliness and drew yet more blood until her agitation subsided and she went slack again.

"I shall come back this evening," he promised.

Andrei was laid to rest the next day. My parents had arrived from the country, my brother, Vanya, from his regiment, and together with the other mourners—all but Xenia—we set out just before dawn, our heads veiled, and followed his hearse on foot through sleeping streets. We approached the church, its spires black against a watery sky streaked with red, like bloody rags. The bells began to toll the dirge, from high to low, the last knell so deep it entered the bones.

Inside, the full Imperial choir had gathered to sing the service for their fallen brother. Even Count Razumovsky, together with his brother Ivan, was in attendance. Xenia might have been happy to see Andrei so honored, I thought, and close at the heels of this thought followed the worry that I had not laid in sufficient provisions to feed so many afterwards.

The choir began the Kathisma hymn for the dead, their solemn chants reverberating in the stony air. I listened for a void made by the absence of Andrei's voice, but in truth I could not hear it. I then fell into the stupor that comes with long and familiar rites and emerged only when the priest called the mourners to the last embrace.

*Come ye, therefore, let us kiss him who was but lately with us; for he is committed to the grave; he is covered with a stone; he taketh up his abode in the gloom, and is interred among the dead.*

I have heard it remarked by foreigners, in particular the English, that our mourning is a cacophony compared with their own more muted grief. I remember Gaspari once said that not even the warm-blooded Italians make such a noise as Russians. Our serfs rend their garments and pull their hair, nor is it thought unmanly to weep. Even by the measure of our own customs, though, the grief for Andrei was loud.

He made a handsome corpse. Across his forehead lay the crown, a paper band with lettering that petitioned God's mercy on his soul. But for this, one might have thought he was only sleeping off a night of immoderate pleasure rather than a life of it. I kissed him good-bye.

We emerged from the church, blinking into a day gone bright as a mirror. The sounds of sleigh bells and laughter rang in the thin air, for it was Christmastide. We seemed out of step with the calendar, sealed up in a private and unseasonable grief. I pondered the strangeness of this, that his death could rend to pieces the little sphere I lived in, yet leave no mark on the world beyond. Merrymakers, seeing our solemn procession to the cemetery, crossed themselves, but we did not dampen their revelry. It was considered good luck to be passed by a funeral procession, and they would not see in the open coffin a picture of their own ends.

As for the supper after, it was little different from others but for the absence of the widow, who lay upstairs. Cleansed by their tears, the mourners ate and drank heartily. Silently, they raised their glasses to Andrei's empty chair with its glass of vodka and black bread.

# Unloosing the Material World

## CHAPTER EIGHT

I found I could feed Xenia by pressing a spoon to her lips till they opened, ladling in a bit of broth, retrieving the spoon, and holding her jaw shut till she swallowed. It required the unflagging persistence of a mother bird. I took Andrei's place in their bed that I might look after her, and my sleep was as restless as it had been when we were children and last shared a bed. Muffled sobs seeped into my dreams, along with muttered sounds that might have been words. Once, she cried out, "Blood! Blood!" her voice choked with anguish. When I tried to rouse her, she clutched blindly at my arm. "There is so much greed in the world." She keened and mewled but could not be roused from sleep, and in the morning she was just as she had been, vacant-eyed and mute. Then one night I awoke and felt her watching me.

"How long has it been?" The voice, though feeble, was her own.

"A week and some. A week and two days."

"You've returned, then."

I answered that I had not left, except to go out for necessity.

"*Moy solovushka,*" she whispered.

It was her pet name for Andrei, "my nightingale." I thought she was asking for him, and I was loath to tell her again what had broken her in the first place. I cast about for some way to couch the truth in gentleness or avoid it altogether.

"Do you suffer?" she asked.

Her gaze seemed directed behind me, and I looked there. The room was black and still, and I could see nothing. It came to me then: it is on the ninth day after death that the soul is said to leave the body. On the fortieth day, it departs this world. Between these two points lies a blank space that the Church does not account for, but peasants will tell you that the soul returns home and takes up residence behind the stove. She thought he was in the room with us.

My senses stretched taut against the darkness. Her breath caught. And released. Caught, caught again, then released, thick with tears.

"I thought it would be me," she rasped. "Not you."

Over the following days I tried to draw her out from her trance, talking on whatever subject came into my head. I shaped my discourse round familiar things, reminding her of times from our girlhood—the day she had fallen into the river, the bonfires built by the villagers to celebrate Shrovetide, the elephant that carried the jester and his wife—anything I could think that might spark some recognition in her face. I sometimes fancied she was listening, but she might only have been entranced by the movement of my lips or the sound of my voice.

Then, one afternoon, I suggested that the bedchamber might use a little airing. Struggling with the latch on the window, I pried it open. The bright smell of fresh snow washed into the room. "There, that's better, don't you think?"

"Ice." The word popped out like a cork from a bottle.

Delighted, I encouraged her further. "Have you slept well?"

"Ice."

"On the window?"

"The step. I was very cold."

"Do you want me to close it up again?" She showed no comprehension, so I indicated the glass. "Shall I shut the window?"

"I am dead."

I startled. During the past weeks I had sometimes had this very thought, that when Andrei died, she had died with him and had left behind a breathing corpse.

"You have been very near it," I said, "but God has seen fit to bring you back to us."

She took in the room slowly, as if she were at pains to recall it. Then her eyes lighted on me and recognition pierced her. Her features contracted with agony.

"You were at the palace. You saw what happened."

"Yes."

She waited for more.

"He fell down the steps and struck his head."

She nodded as if to say she knew this much already.

"He didn't suffer," I assured her. "He fell and was gone."

Her eyes drifted to the window and rested there for so long a time that I thought she had returned to her mute state. I was on the verge of slipping out when she asked, "Was he confessed and given the last sacraments?"

I had to admit that, no, he had died too suddenly.

Her eyes shut. "He was not ready." Her voice was flat. "In the dream, it was me. It should have been."

SHE AWAKENED AS IF SHE had indeed been dead. But the person who returned to the world was not Xenia. Grief had unyoked her from herself. Dull-eyed, like an animal in extremis, she looked on her surroundings and her loved ones with indifference. Or she might suddenly begin to weep, even to tear at her nightclothes, but what emotions passed over her were like leaves borne on the surface of a river and caught in swirling eddies, unattached to anything visible.

Her speech, too, was oddly disjointed and followed no definite course. I might say a thing to her and she would answer me sensibly only to say another thing so discordant that I was thrown into confusion. Sometimes I would hear her talking in her room, and, answering as I came, find that I had been mistaken, had caught one voice of a private conversation and believed it addressed to me. In truth she had been talking to Andrei.

She did not leave her bed, and then one day I found her in the icon corner of her room, prostrate, and as feeble as if she had crawled across the steppes. This became her practice. She would kneel there for long hours, even through the length of the night, without slippers or a shawl, her gaze fixed on the image of the Virgin of Vladimir and seemingly in prayer. I say "seemingly" because, except that she had moved from her bed to the floor, the distinction between this state and her former oblivion was too subtle to observe. Her mournful appearance and drooping, shadowy eyes were so like the Virgin's that they might have been reflected in a mirror.

Before the death of her child, she had not been devout beyond the ordinary, keeping the fasts and praying when it was right to do so and no more. But now, while the rest of the world celebrated Shrovetide, Xenia crossed early into a most extreme observation of Lent. She not only prayed but also fasted like a monk, taking only tiny morsels of bread and these only if I chided her. "You must eat if you would recover your health," I insisted, but she was less pliable now than when I had spoon-fed her. "I do not wish to recover it," she answered.

The Great Lent came to the rest of us in its customary time. On the first day, the house was readied, the rugs taken up, the curtains and shutters taken down, and everything scrubbed. Marfa and Masha went from room to room with a kettle and a copper bowl into which had been placed a hot brick and dried mint leaves. Pouring water over the hissing brick, they waved the medicinal steam under the beds and into each corner to chase out the wicked spirit of Lady Shrovetide. The good dishes and silver candlesticks were put away, and old sheeting was thrown over the pictures and furniture that we might forget earthly pleasures and prepare our spirits to fast. As custom dictated, we put on our oldest patched clothes and made to go to church.

Xenia surprised us by coming downstairs and professing the desire to go also. She had dressed herself, putting on light clothes unsuited to the season. In the six weeks since Andrei's death, she had so wasted that they hung loose as sacking on her. Her pale hair was undone and floating about her head, her feet were bare—all this conspired to give her the appearance of a wraith and not a woman of twenty-six years.

"Xenichka, you are not well enough," I said, but she had no care for her health, and when Ivan opened the front door she ran out into the snow on bare feet. She could not be persuaded by reason to return inside, not even to dress properly. I finally relented and had Masha bring stockings, shoes, and outer garments out to the sleigh. "Keep this about you," I said, wrapping her in a fur pelisse. I put her feet into shoes and took her purse, which she had stuffed heavy with coins, that she might put her thin hands into a muff.

I blame myself. I should have bid Grishka carry her inside and sit guard at the door rather than take her with us. In the last hour of the service, she did not rise up from the prostrations and lay with her forehead resting on the cold stone floor. Looks and whispers were directed at her, but no matter; after the service I had more cause than this to rue my mistake.

Outside the church, a throng of beggars, the poor and

those others whom we call blessed, were gathered to receive alms. The feeble and lame lay on the ground from
the doors to the street, and those who were able-bodied
crowded close round the emerging worshippers and murmured their supplications.

The sight of these beggars revived Xenia. She slipped
from my supporting arm, took back her purse, and began
to thread her way amongst the unfortunates, exchanging
handfuls of coins for their blessings.

*"Signorina."* A strange and gawky man in boots and a
heavy fur cloak bowed to me, wishing me good morning.
It was the musico Gaspari. Without paint, his features were
almost plain, and I would not have known him except for
his accent.

"I wish to offer you my sorrow." The lilting voice was
disconcertingly at odds with this likeness of a man.

"Thank you. You were most kind on that terrible night."

He demurred, shaking his head.

"Did you stay on that night and pray over him?"

"I cannot read the Russian prayers, *signorina.* But yes, I
stayed." He clutched his cloak closer about him to ward off
the cold.

Not only his appearance but also his manner was changed
from our first meeting. To be sure, none of us is the same
person at church as at a party, but without the trappings of
female garb he seemed less in command of his person. The
Roman goddess at the masquerade had been witty, even
haughty, but this pallid creature was so undistinguished
that even his extreme height did not lend him presence.

"His wife, Xenia Grigoryevna . . ." A delicate hand started to flutter and then, deprived of a fan, wilted. "I saw her inside. She is recovered?"

I looked about but did not see her. "She is not yet well but is better than she was."

"I may call on her?"

From habit, I replied that she would be grateful, though in truth she certainly would not. She had received no one since Andrei's death. I looked about for the sleigh, thinking that perhaps she was waiting in it, and I might get away. Near the street, a knot of people had gathered round a half-naked woman, one of the *klikushi* who are possessed by demons and are often taken with fits when they visit a church. Then I saw I was mistaken. It was Xenia.

When I got to her, she was trying to remove her chemise, but her fingers trembled so that she could not undo the laces. I grabbed her hands to still them. "Are you mad?"

"I am out of coins," she said. Her voice quaked from cold, but otherwise she seemed unperturbed.

Looking for something to cover her, I saw the trail of her clothing, each garment now in the possession of a beggar—her skirt covering the lap of an old woman, and beyond that her shoes and overshoes, the fur pelisse and its matching muff, and so on to the empty coin purse.

I snatched the pelisse back and wrapped it round her shoulders. "Would you freeze to death? Is that your wish?"

She considered this; the prospect did not seem to disturb her.

## CHAPTER NINE

That Lenten season, I had no need of bells to call me to prayer nor icons to put me in mind of our Savior's suffering. I had Xenia. Very early every morning, she set forth to matins. I went with her, but my own piety was a fraud, compelled as it was by apprehension of what she might say or do were I not there to prevent it.

Before leaving the house, she stuffed her purse with kopeks and silver rubles she had taken from the household strongbox and filled a basket with bread she had taken from the kitchen. These she distributed to the unfortunates outside the church, who began to greet her by calling her *matushka*, "little mother." As she emptied her purse and basket, she drew from them stories of how they had come to their situation, labyrinthine tales of illness and death, lost positions, failed crops, violent or cheating masters. Once when I was late in rising, she had already gone, and when I arrived at the church, I found her sitting on the ground in the company of the beggars, quite as though she meant to set out a begging bowl herself.

More respectable persons kept a discreet distance. Her look barred their approach, and those few who braved addressing her were rewarded with disinterest or, worse, her unmodified thoughts. A singer in the choir who had regarded himself as a rival to Andrei tendered his condolences to Xenia. He heaped extravagant praise on her husband and claimed a great affection for him.

Xenia cut him off. "You were jealous of him."

"It was I who brought the largest wreath for his casket," the man protested. "I might have expected a word of thanks."

"You already have your reward. He is dead."

Feeling the eyes of those round us, I hurried her into the church. "You should not have done that."

"His compliments were lies. He showed no affection to Andrei while he lived."

"He meant no harm," I answered. "It is what people say when someone has died."

She slapped my hand from her shoulder. "What do I care about that?"

When she was safely in prayer beside me, I tried to turn my mind to God but I could not, except in anger. *Is this what you want,* I demanded, *that she should wreck herself so publicly?*

After the service, she asked again to be taken to Smolenskoye cemetery. She had not yet been to his grave, for I had feared it might further unhinge her, but plainly I had no power to protect her from herself.

"As you wish," I replied.

Her eyes sharpened inquisitively.

Yes, I knew the pettiness of my tone, the martyred weariness, but I thought myself justified in it.

For all my misgivings, the cemetery did not disturb her. She did not even weep at the sight of his grave but stood looking on the new stone and the raised mound of snow as though she were absorbing the truth of them. Then she sat right down on the ground beside his head. She ran her fingers over the letters of his name. After a while, she said, "Leave us."

I hesitated. "I will wait in the sleigh." She did not answer.

She was gone so long that I began to worry and to repent my former harshness, but at last she appeared from out of the trees and without a word climbed into the sleigh. I could not read anything in her countenance; she was only quiet.

THE LARGE CIRCLE OF ANDREI and Xenia's friends who had called at the house after little Katenka's death kept away now, as though so much sorrow and ill fortune were a contagion. I do not fault them. Had she been receptive to their sympathy then, she might have had it now. No matter; she did not want it. She would not receive even her own mother. After that incident, a friend of Aunt Galya's would not be put off by my saying that Xenia was indisposed to visitors and insisted on going upstairs, since Xenia would not come down. "She only thinks she wants solitude," said this woman whose name I have forgotten. She knew what it was to mourn a husband, the woman said, "but trust me, too much solitude is the worst cure." Finding Xenia in her room, she tried to comfort her with assurances that this grief would pass.

"I thought I should have died with my husband," Madam Somethingorother said. "Nothing could console me. My appetite suffered, and I took no pleasure from my friends. I could not be amused. Then one day"—the widow's round face brightened at the memory—"I was brought a little china dish of strawberries and cream. Eating them, I thought I had never tasted anything so lovely. And after that, all my old delights returned to me, one by one."

Xenia looked at her, impassive. "So you believe I may also become an idiot again?"

This is not to say we were entirely without company. Gaspari was insensible to her slights. The first time he called, she happened to wander into the drawing room shortly after him. She was wearing Andrei's jacket, a habit she had acquired that seemed to comfort her. He stood and bowed, and she perused his person.

"Are you the eunuch?"

He answered with no sign that the question was rude. Thus encouraged, she sat down beside him. "Did it hurt when they cut you?"

"I do not remember it. I was given opium."

"My heart has been cut out of me, yet I still feel such pain."

He nodded. "There is no opium for this wound," he said, touching his breast. "I am sorry for the loss of your husband."

With matching graveness, she replied, "And I am sorry for the loss of your eggs." They sat together without speaking for another few moments and then, abruptly, she stood. "I must return to my prayers." And with this, she turned and left the room.

When he took his leave, he presented his card and asked me to extend to her his apologies for having come at an inopportune hour, promising to try again for a more agreeable time.

We were host as well to increasing numbers of beggars. Though Xenia was discourteous to her friends, she took exceeding care of those beneath her, and those most in need she brought back to the house with us. She offered them food and a place to sleep and whatever else they expressed a desire for. One cannot fault such behavior; those who have read the *Domostroi* will recognize that these acts conform exactly to its prescriptions for Christian charity. That said, so literal an interpretation was exasperating. Many of these unfortunates were pulsing with fleas and stank so strongly that Marfa would not tolerate their sleeping in the servants' room. I tried to make Xenia see reason. Where were we to put them? Her answer was to bed the worst offenders in front of the stove in the drawing room that they might be out of the way, and to have their food brought there also. The stench could never be aired entirely from that room, but as we no longer had respectable visitors, it was, I suppose, a moot concern.

More troubling than what came into the house was what left it. I discovered that in addition to the bread, Xenia had been tucking into her basket whatever other thing caught her eye—the porcelain bonbonniere on her dressing table, a silvered candlestick. I could not curb her generosity. I tried bargaining her down to sensible sacrifices—an apple in place of the inkwell, an earthenware mug for a porcelain cup—but the ploy failed, and so I began to hide certain of her more precious things, reasoning that she might otherwise regret later having given them away.

One day, she pulled from the basket a particularly fine pair of gloves and handed them to an orphan. They were made of delicate white kid worked with silver thread, and I had coveted them once. When the child pulled them onto her filthy hands, I flinched.

"Xenia, if you must, it would be better to sell the finer things and then give the profits to the poor."

She didn't answer but looked on me with something like pity. I felt that she could read my thoughts.

"They are too thin," I protested. "They will not even keep her hands warm."

Perhaps it was to appease me that some days later she determined to pack up her court dresses and the rest of her finery and take them to a pawn shop. Heaped on the bed and floor was a colorful froth of skirts and bodices.

"Oh no, darling, I did not mean that you should sell these," I said.

"I cannot stand the sight of them."

"Maybe not now . . ." Someday, I thought, she would come out of mourning and return to society. She would want to marry again. I started to pick up a matching bodice and skirt, yellow brocade with gold lace trim, that I might return them to the wardrobe. "Later, you may think differently."

"She is *gone!*" Xenia shrieked. "Are you too dull to see it? There is no point in keeping her things."

She snatched the bodice from my hands and in doing so tore loose a piece of lace. Fiercely, she ripped it away from the sleeve and then tore the lace from the other sleeve for good measure. She grabbed up two handfuls of the skirt, meaning to rend this to pieces also, but the fabric would not give. Her features strained with the effort and then went slack, and quick as the storm had erupted it was spent, and she was overcome with remorse.

"I'm sorry." She held the skirt back out to me. "Please take it. You should have something pretty to wear when your husband calls."

"I do not need your dresses or your pity either."

She nodded and let it fall to the floor. "You are right to be offended. I should not try to buy your forgiveness with rubbish. You see its worth. Oh, Dasha"—her face contorted in anguish—"when I recall my terrible thoughtlessness. I have let people starve that I might wear that lace." She looked about her. "But I shall be naked before God. How shall I ever account for all this?"

The pawnbroker was more than willing to relieve her of her finery. Fingering a pink moiré silk, he tried to mask his greed with appraising looks, frowning at imaginary flaws and clucking. After thus inspecting each dress, he offered a very small sum for the lot, less than the worth of one alone.

Xenia was content to take whatever he offered, but I would not allow it and haggled with the miser. He raised his price a little, then seeing Xenia's disinterest in the outcome of our bargaining returned his attention to her.

"I can see that you know the worth of discretion. It is worth more than money, and I can promise you, no one shall know where these came from. I will be a cipher, a stone."

She was as impassive as the Sphinx in reply.

Only by irritating him like a fly was I able to extract another fifty kopeks. From the shop to the church, I vented my annoyance at her having been swindled, but I could not persuade Xenia to share my grievance. She was as blasé about money as the Empress herself. When we reached the church, she handed the profits, purse and all, to the first beggar who held out his hand.

GASPARI CALLED AGAIN, AND AGAIN Xenia was at her prayers but said that I should entertain him in her place. Had he relied on me for this, we should have sat in silence. I am often tongue-tied with strangers and have what the philosopher Monsieur Diderot calls *l'esprit de l'escalier*, staircase wit: only long after a remark is made to me will my imagination supply the thing I should have said in reply. But I was further stricken with self-consciousness by Gaspari. There were no rules by which to steer conversation with a person who was neither man nor woman.

As it happened, though, Gaspari liked to talk, and even hampered by his poor Russian he was gifted at this. Left to choose a theme, he told me of his village in the north of Italy and described for me its varied charms—hillsides dotted with sheep, a sun that shone far warmer than it does here, the scents of rosemary and drying grasses that perfume the air.

"My mother's garden has a fig tree in it," he said, "and to eat one of these figs is to taste music on the tongue. I dream of this, to sit in the warm sun and eat a plate of these figs."

I nodded.

He flattered me that I had a talent to listen. "Most persons, they are intent only to make the impression. But you are not this way. I see you at the ball; you do not care for what you look like, only to help your cousin."

"I was mortified," I admitted.

"I do not know this word."

"Embarrassed."

"Ah." He nodded. "Mortified. It is the condition of life, yes?"

I gradually forgot my discomfort and even came to anticipate his next visit. If Xenia did not show herself—and she rarely did—he was content to pass an hour entertaining me with accounts of who had attended his performance on the previous night, what they had worn and said, who had snubbed or flattered whom. A keen mimic, he would adopt the guttural voice of a well-known attaché and this man's habit of adjusting the weight of his stomach as he spoke, and then with the next breath he would answer in a comical falsetto that I recognized as belonging to a certain lady-in-waiting.

I confess, I wondered at first if Xenia might be fodder for amusement on his subsequent calls—she would be so easy to mock. I did not know how few doors were open to him, how alone he was in Russia. But more important, I did not know then how Gaspari judged the world, upside down. His barbed wit was reserved for his betters; those whom the rest of the world disdained he treated with courtesy. I think this accounted for the tolerance he showed to Xenia. When I apologized for her, he assured me there was no need.

"She is herself," he said.

Though I could not agree, I did not correct him.

XENIA AND I CONTINUED TO work at cross-purposes, she pillaging her possessions and I hiding what of them I could in my room. Her methods were haphazard: when I went with her to Andrei's grave, I might find small tokens she had left there on a previous visit—a swollen folio of music and the glass stopper that had belonged to a decanter—and I could only guess at what else may have been taken away by grave robbers. On one day, she went to the church with only an onion and a linen rag, but on the next she pulled from her basket pieces of silver that had been put away for Lent, handing a soupspoon to a bewildered beggar and a fork to the next. Coming to a lean man with leather skin and a beard so ratty it appeared to grow uninterrupted from his sheepskin, she fished about in the basket. She dug out something but then stopped short of giving it. Her eyes softened. "It is such a little thing," she mused, turning the object in her palm. "The material world is so strong, Dasha.

These things are worth nothing, yet they cling to my soul like vines."

I recognized Andrei's bone-handled shaving razor. It had been her morning habit to shave him with this. I imagine his hand was often not sufficiently steady to do it for himself, but she had also cherished this intimate ceremony between them and would caress his smoothed cheek and linger over the dimpled thumbprint above his lip. Now, she unhinged the blade and studied it. A cold fear seized me, and had she been a child I would have snatched the blade from her. But I could not do this. I watched as she put her forefinger to the edge. A scarlet thread appeared, and she looked at it without curiosity. After a long moment, she closed the razor and pressed it upon the beggar. "It is yours now. Take care with it," she said.

In spite of what she said, most of her possessions seemed to have no hold on her whatsoever. She emptied her own wardrobe of even the undergarments. Other necessaries went missing. Marfa grumbled that she had no ladle for the soup. When I went to mend a stocking, the thimble was gone from the sewing basket, and one night the chamber pot was missing from under our bed. I felt about for it, increasingly discomfited, went into my room and discovered its chamber pot was gone also. At last I had need to stumble down the stairs and out into the frozen yard to relieve myself in the privy.

The mystery of one chamber pot's disappearance was solved the next day when I saw this same article sitting on the church step. A fool whom Xenia had brought home two days prior was using it to collect coins. I was furious. "It's all right," Xenia assured me. "She did not steal it. I gave it to her."

"It is *not* all right," I fumed, and beside myself with anger, I snatched it up and, upturning it, showered coins into the fool's lap. "It is not, not, *not* all right, Xenia." I fled, still clutching the chamber pot until I had rounded the corner, where I threw it down and it shattered on the cobble.

One day, Marfa came to me and asked me to speak to her mistress. The servants were loath to disturb her solitude—whether out of courtesy or fear that she might fling something at them, I cannot say. "I would not trouble her, but there's the matter of flour."

"What of it?"

"There isn't any. And the miller won't put any more on credit without some payment."

It turned out not to be so simple a matter as flour. When I looked, there was also no salt or lard and very little of anything else. Even by the spare measure of Lent, the provisions in the larder were meager: small handfuls of this and that, a single onion, a crock of pickled cabbage, a hard sausage that could not be eaten till Easter. Marfa was anxious to account for herself. "What with all the extra mouths," she explained, "I have twice asked her for money, but she is too much distracted to remember."

"Just make do with what's here," I said. "I'll speak to her, but we can go for one day without bread."

Marfa looked doubtful, and it came out that it was not only the miller who was owed.

I interrupted Xenia at her prayers, or what seemed to be prayers; as she did not speak them aloud, it was impossible to know with certainty.

"I'm sorry to disturb you, but I have need of money to settle some debts. It seems we owe all over town."

She did not answer or give any sign that she had heard me.

"If you will lend me the key to the strongbox, I will get it myself."

Again, there was no response. She was not being pious, I thought, but obstinate, and I determined to stand and wait until she acknowledged me, no matter how long that might be. It was not as if I were asking her to go round to these creditors herself, or to bake the bread or help with the washing. Looking on her back side, I reflected on the times she had left me to answer for her to callers, and to speak in a whisper so as not to disturb her. The servants went about on tiptoe and let the carpets collect dust rather than make a noise by beating them. Yet she could not be bothered in return to concern herself in the slightest with her own household.

Perhaps sensing that I would not go away, she spoke. "Can it not wait?"

"Not unless you can multiply loaves and fishes."

She rose from her knees. Feeling about in a drawer, she produced a small iron key, went to the strongbox, and turned the key in its lock.

"Take what you need," she said, and returned to the icon corner and knelt again.

Except for some papers in the bottom, the box was empty.

"Take what? Where is the rest?"

She regarded me with weariness. "What remains?"

"In here? Nothing. That is what I am telling you." I turned the box upside down to demonstrate, and a single sheet of paper fluttered to the floor. "Is there some other place where Andrei kept money?" He was not poor. Besides a good salary, he had received lavish sums from the Empress and Count Razumovsky. Andrei and Xenia had never wanted for luxuries. "Perhaps in his desk or dressing table?"

She said nothing, but the blankness of her expression answered for her.

I thought back on the handfuls of coins I had seen her give away over the past month, and realized with horror that together with what had escaped my observation, the total sum of them might be anything.

"So there is nothing more?" I could not make myself believe it.

"Here." She handed me the paper.

"What is this?"

"The deed to the house."

"And what would you have me do with it?"

"Sell it."

"To buy flour? Don't be absurd, Xenia." I thrust the paper back into her hand. "If you sell your house, where shall you live?"

"Our Savior lived without a house."

"That is all fine and well, but what of the souls He has entrusted to you? Where shall they live? Or would you sell them, too?" I asked. "It is not only beggars in the street who depend on your charity, Xenia." As I said it, I was not unmindful that I was included in this company.

"We have eaten today, and we shall eat again tomorrow." She said this just as a child might, her face empty of any anxiety.

Something changed for me in that moment. Confronted with the empty strongbox and its promise of ruin, together with her complacency . . . I left her there and went from room to room with rising agitation, looking for something I might sell.

I felt like a thief, but one who has come to a house already robbed. How had I not seen it? Xenia had succeeded in removing most everything that would fit in her basket. I went to my room and looked over the meager hoard I had hidden away. The cloisonné clock. The jeweled earbobs that were her wedding present from Andrei. Little Katenka's christening gown and cross. No, these were too precious to be sold. I settled on a brass candlestick chased with silver, half of the pair that had graced the sideboard. This I took to the wretched pawnbroker. It fetched sixty kopeks, just enough to appease the miller and fishmonger, but not the greengrocer. And we would need more wood for the pile and dried fruits for the Easter *kulich*. I returned to his shop with the clock and sold him the sideboard as well, and these bought provisions sufficient to last through the Easter feast.

Never in my life before or since have I awaited that day with such hunger. Dry as a raisin, some part of me still hoped nonetheless. Xenia's desolation had so entwined with the Lenten season that she seemed an enlargement of its mood, almost as though she were an actor in a Passion play. I anticipated that with the arrival of Easter she would doff her mourning. It was Xenia's resurrection I awaited.

At the midnight service, the chants poured into my soul like water, and as the light was passed from taper to taper, I felt my spirits lift on the rising glow. The holy doors were thrown open and we spilt out into the night and circled the church. Buoyed on an upwelling of joy, with the hundreds of voices around me in song, with the tumultuous pealing of the bells, I was exultant. The priest proclaimed, *Christ is risen*, and every voice answered fervently, *Truly He is risen!*

Together with Gaspari and a mother and child whom Xenia had found outside the church, we returned afterwards to the house lit bright and the table laden with food and decorated with pussy willows and flowers. The servants were happy to the edge of tears, and we exchanged colored eggs with kisses on the cheek. I gave Xenia her egg, kissing her thrice. She did not crack it but put it instead into her basket to be given to the poor. When Gaspari also presented her with an egg, she reciprocated by withdrawing mine from her basket for him. He was on the point of cracking it, but then stopped and handed it back, gesturing that she should return it to the basket.

Vodka was poured out and, raising my glass, I inhaled it like a clean, sharp draught of winter air. I have never felt such thirst, such hunger. We ate the *kulich*, the paskha, the lamb. It was wonderful. There were eggs and more eggs, wine and more vodka, and I ate and drank as though I had fasted for a year.

Xenia ate nothing but seemed content to sit at table and collect eggs. Several times throughout the meal, I saw Gaspari repeat this ritual of giving her an egg, accepting another in return, and then handing it back to her. At last, I thought to peek under the table and saw her basket on the floor beside her chair, heaped with red eggs as well as pieces of *kulich*.

The table was strewn with egg peelings and walnut shells, the plates wiped clean but for bits of gristle and bone. I was sated, heavy-limbed, and light-headed. Across the table, Gaspari stood. With no more preface than this, he clasped his hands at his breast, rested his gaze above our heads, and parted his lips.

The air was pierced with a startling sound, high and clear and powerful. The sound expanded and held for an impossibly long time before gliding to the next note and the next. He seemed not to breathe but only to exhale music, warbling and sliding over vowels and consonants as endlessly as water rounds over stones in a shallow stream.

How may one describe enchantment? As he sang, his countenance softened, and without benefit of costume or any other artifice of the stage, the Gaspari I knew faded and was transformed into something eerily beautiful. A delicate hand, rising and turning like a vine, seemed to unfurl this otherworldly sound into the air. Though I could not translate the words, there was no need, for the sound went straight to my soul, transcending the poor and broken language we mortals must use. I slipped gratefully out of my body and floated on the current of music, feeling that all of us round the table were a single spirit, a single being. I was filled with such love. The voice soared, wave upon wave, until the last note, quivering with tenderness, put us ashore again too soon.

The musici have since fallen out of favor, and I do not expect to hear such an ethereal sound again until the angels sing me home. It is just as well. Such radiance was not intended for mortals, and to achieve it, hundreds of boys were mutilated, made into monsters so that a few among the wounded might sing. That such beauty should come from such suffering . . . I see it in Xenia also. It is a terrible mystery.

The next morning, I awoke to stabbing light and the sound of church bells ringing, each clang so deafening that I might have been trapped within the bell itself, with the bronze tongue striking my skull. Anyone may ring the bells in Bright Week and so they rang incessantly, as I foresaw they would for days yet. Coupled with this misery, in the previous days the ice on the Neva had begun to break up, and in the lulls between chimes I heard the river's painful groans, the screech of ice against ice. Against this noise, the promises of spring and our Lord's resurrection seemed faint abstractions, and the bliss of Gaspari's voice an improbable memory.

Xenia was in her accustomed place in the corner, her

black shape bent before the Virgin of Vladimir. She was as still as a corpse, her countenance empty, her eyes sunken in shadow. Apparently, I had missed the morning service, but Xenia had not: the basket she had filled with red eggs the night before sat next to her, empty.

I saw the truth of our situation with the clarity of a drunkard's remorse. There was nothing left in the larder, and I would have to sell the sleigh and horse.

## CHAPTER TEN

That same week, Nadya and her mother came to call and brought with them intricately painted eggs, one for Xenia and another for myself.

"Xenia is at her prayers just now," I said, "but she will be delighted by this."

Aunt Galya smiled thinly and held fast to the egg meant for Xenia. "We can wait till she is finished. I should very much like to give it to her myself."

I showed them into the drawing room, grateful as I did that I had not yet found it necessary to sell the chairs, or Xenia to give them away. The sideboard was gone, but the divan and two chairs remained.

They glanced about, poorly concealing their dismay. "A house always looks barren at Lent," Aunt Galya remarked. "But why have you not put things back in their places?"

Nadya answered her. "Xenia has become a great benefactress, Maman. Isn't that so, Dasha?"

I nodded. "She is very kind to the poor. They call her *Matushka*."

Nadya looked as though she had eaten something bitter. "So kind she has given them even the clothes from her back?"

"Just the once."

A look passed between mother and daughter, and Nadya made her aspect more pleasing. "Let us speak freely. Like sisters. My mother and I are greatly concerned for her. People are talking. Yesterday, it came back to us that she had been seen giving her corset to a person on the street."

I turned the egg in my palm. On one side was painted the head of our Savior, his eyes two dark and elongated hollows of sorrow. The reverse showed a pastoral scene, a young lord and lady courting in a glade, she perched on a swing and he pushing her.

Aunt Galya put an affectionate hand on my shoulder. "I know you love her and would protect her, Dasha, but consider that you are protecting her from those who love her equally as well. Clearly, she is troubled, and we want to help."

The promise of help overruled my scruples, and I spilt all the trials of the past weeks, how Xenia had emptied the strongbox, how one moment she was taciturn and the next was taking me to task for putting a portion of sausage on her plate. "She eats only bread now and too little of that. She has no appetite for anything but prayer. *That* she may do for hours. You may as well know that there is no point to waiting on her. She will not come down."

Nadya was horrified. "She can't have given away everything?"

"Not all," I admitted. "I hid some things from her."

"But the strongbox . . . is all her money gone, then?"

I said that it was, except for the few kopeks that remained from the sale of the sideboard. If Nadya might speak to Kuzma Zakharovich about a loan, I began, but her outraged look silenced me.

Aunt Galya was also distressed at her daughter's misfortune. But she knew what it was to lose a husband and all one's possessions, and perhaps it was this that made her better able to school her emotions.

"What did you hide, Dasha?"

"It is only that I thought she may desire them later."

She nodded approvingly and encouraged me to list for her the various items, which I did.

"Odds and ends," Nadya fumed.

A look of reproof passed from mother to daughter. "There are still the serfs. And the house and furnishings," Aunt Galya said. "But she can't be allowed to go on like this. We must do what is best for her, however hard."

The following week, Xenia was served with a summons to show herself in court and answer to the charge that she was alienated, startled out of her mind. If she were found unfit to manage her own affairs, she would be declared one of the *sumasbrodnye*, mad, then dispossessed of her property and given into the custody of her family.

It may be that they were indeed trying to save Xenia from herself. Still, the word itself was shocking. For all her strangeness, I could not reconcile Xenia with that word. If she behaved rashly, well, had she not always been passionate and a bit wild? It was only her profound sorrow that made her like a foreigner amongst us now. Even stripping to her skin on the steps of the church might be deemed an excess of grief. True, I had never seen grief like this, but neither had I known anyone so completely possessed by love of her husband. One could not expect such passion, when ripped from its source, to fade gently. Given time, I thought, the wound might yet heal.

Xenia received the news of the summons with no visible concern. She wished only to return to her room, and when I expressed surprise that she could be so indifferent to her own fate, she asked if there was something else I would have her do.

IT BEING COMMON FOR PERSONS to attempt to seize the property of their relations by falsely declaring them mad, all such cases bypassed the lower courts and were brought directly before the Senate. Thus, on the appointed day, we appeared at the long expanse of red and white buildings that make up the Twelve Colleges and were directed to a vast anteroom. It was teeming with persons, many more than the benches lining the walls would accommodate.

All who had business with the crown were gathered here like waters behind a dike and trickled through a single set of doors. Amongst these were foreign ambassadors hoping to influence the Senate to favor a trade agreement, nobles awaiting civilian appointments or promotions in rank, and merchants seeking military contracts or the rights to sell vodka. Those appealing the ruling of a lower court or seeking criminal review were also funneled here. And one must presume there were other persons in the room like Xenia, who might or might not be ruled mad.

Those petitioners without influence or means to bribe their way through these doors might well linger in the shallows for ten or even twenty years without their suits being heard, and this prospect was reflected in their behaviors. Like the denizens of Hades, they sat or stood in attitudes suggesting they had taken up residence here long ago and had since forgotten the manners of the other world. They scratched themselves freely, yawned, and even slept with their chins on their chests and their mouths gaping. Some had withdrawn so far into themselves that they resembled Xenia; others, more social, played at games of dice or cards and made such a noise that clerks who appeared at intervals to call forward the next case could not be heard above the din. The residents, apparently having lost hope of hearing their own names called, paid them no mind. Looking about, I wondered how a judge might sort the mad from the rest.

Kuzma Zakharovich found us in the midst of this crowd. He wished me good morning and then greeted Xenia in a louder tone as if she might be deaf. She gave him in return a penetrating look, which discomfited him.

"Does she not speak?" he asked me.

"If she is so inclined, but she cannot be depended upon for courtesy."

He gave her another wary glance. "My wife and Galina Stepanovna are anxious of her whereabouts," he said, and bid us join them.

Aunt Galya had not seen Xenia since Andrei's death. "So thin and bleak," she exclaimed, kissing her. "The Lord gave you such prettiness and only to take it away like this. My poor daughter."

A hardly noticeable twitch unsettled Xenia's features, as if her mother's kiss were a fly lighting on her cheek.

"When we are through here," Aunt Galya went on, "we shall take you home with us and see that you are properly tended to."

"You see how she is," Nadya said. "Your affection is wasted on her. It would be just as well to send her to a monastery."

"You want feeling, Nadya, to say such things now."

All of Kuzma Zakharovich's remaining influence must have been wielded to turn the wheels of Justice, for Xenia's case was called that same afternoon, and we were ushered past the residents and through the doors, and to a smaller chamber. A judge and a scribe sat behind a long table raised on a dais. The judge wore the robe and long, curled wig befitting his office, and the gray complexion of one who has not seen daylight for many years.

The clerk announced the case to His Excellency, who bid the former hunt-master to approach the bench and lay out the matter. This Kuzma Zakharovich did with meticulousness, listing each instance of Xenia's supposed mad behavior as though he were recounting a season of hunts.

"Have you witnessed these things yourself, Gospodin Sudakov, or only heard them reported?" the judge asked.

"I am but the messenger, Your Excellency, but you may see with your own eyes how the woman behaves, in what manner she answers, and judge in your wisdom whether she conforms to the pictures I have painted for you."

"Is this she?" The judge indicated Xenia, and when it was confirmed, he bid her step forward. "Do you understand the charge laid against you?"

She did not speak straightaway. I was anxious lest her silence prove the charge better than all of Kuzma Zakharovich's words, but at last she seemed to find her answer on the floor.

"They say I am mad."

"And how do you answer to this?"

"It would be a comfort."

"Answer in a respectful manner. Are you mad or no?"

She looked up at him. "My reason tells me that my husband and child are dead. I long for less reason."

The judge nodded slowly as she spoke, but it was impossible to read in his face the meaning of these nods.

"Do you understand that should this court find against you, you will not be permitted to marry again? Further, that you shall be remanded to the custody of your nearest relations, and to them shall also go whatever property you may own?"

"It's no matter." She turned and looked directly at her mother and Nadya. "They may have whatever they ask. I do not want it."

"So it seems. Gospodin Sudakov here claims that you have already given the bulk of your property to beggars."

She nodded.

"And are you aware that there is a law against almsgiving?"

She nodded again.

"How do you explain yourself, then?"

There was another long silence.

"You will answer the court."

Xenia looked on him wearily. "I did it that I might give my husband's soul rest. And mine also. But God will not bargain for so little."

"The law is in place to protect Her Imperial Majesty's subjects from charlatans who would prey on their sympathies."

"That your son died was not her fault," Xenia answered. "Her prayers for his soul were well worth thirty kopeks."

The judge was surprised from his dignity. He looked her up and down with undisguised confusion, and an emotion burbling beneath his features threatened to unseat him. He waved the clerk to him. There was a whispered exchange between them that somehow also concerned the person of Kuzma Zakharovich.

At last having satisfied himself, the judge put on again his formal demeanor. He did not look again at Xenia.

"The court cannot condone the breaking of its laws. But if it were to declare mad all those who breached this law, the monasteries should overflow with half of Russia.

"Her speech shows reason, and I can find no cause to declare her *sumasbrodnaya*."

With that, we were dismissed from his presence and other petitioners ushered in behind us.

As we made our way through the anteroom, Kuzma Zakharovich was philosophical. "It is true what they say. Tell God the truth, but give the judge money."

"You might have thought of this before," Nadya said.

"I was given assurances." Kuzma Zakharovich shook his head. "By Prince Tatishchev himself."

"Perhaps the Prince cares less for your welfare than you believe."

At this, Xenia suddenly clutched her sister by the arm and said, "Your husband still lives and wants only your tenderness. Thank God for His mercy!"

Nadya wrenched herself from Xenia's grasp. "You! I will not be preached to by you!" Her harshness caught even the attention of the residents, who left off their other diversions. I was reminded of the festival crowds that stop before a puppet theatre in the street to see Petrushka and his foes knock each other about the head.

"Collect yourself," Aunt Galya said. She then took Xenia's arm and with her free hand turned her daughter's face to meet hers. "You said you would part with whatever we asked. So I will ask it: give up your people and your house, and I shall care for you."

Xenia met her mother's gaze. "If my peasants wish to serve you, they may. But the house is Dasha's. It is my wedding gift to her."

Aunt Galya turned on me, her voice brittle with suspicion. "What is this?"

"I do not know."

"Have you schemed behind my back? After the love I have shown you?"

Someone in the crowd jeered and said I needed whipping.

"I do not deserve to be used so poorly," she said.

I protested my innocence, but she shook me off, fury blooming in her cheeks. "Do not compound your sin with more lies."

# The Musico's Wife

## CHAPTER ELEVEN

We returned from the courthouse even poorer than we had been. The judge had granted Xenia control over what little remained of her estate but at the cost of her family's protection. She, in turn, had bequeathed me this same house as a wedding gift—and with it the enmity of the person charged with finding me a husband. Mine had been a lost cause well before this—I was then nearly twenty-five, well beyond the age of a bride—but I could no longer pretend otherwise.

In short, because it was untenable for us to remain as we were, two women alone and without means or prospects, I devised the only plan I could think of, that we should go to the country and live again under my father's roof. I wrote to him asking that he take us in.

Xenia did not like my plan, though.

"Where shall they go if the door is locked against them?" she asked me.

I explained that Marfa would go to live with her brother;

Ivan and his son, Grishka, to the village where he was born; Masha would be coming with us.

"And the rest?"

"Who?"

"All the others." There was no one unaccounted for. She gestured at the window. "Them."

I understood. She meant the beggars. I answered that they would be taken care of.

She looked at me as though this untruth was a visible blemish on my nose.

"You cannot provide for all the poor, Xenia. You cannot even look after yourself."

"I do not matter," she countered. "But if you stayed here, you might look after them."

"And how shall I do that? I do not have even a kopek to my name."

"God is bringing a husband for you. Then you shall want for nothing."

I could bear it no more. I broke into sobs, and once I had started could not stop myself. Xenia patted and stroked my head, but this only loosened my grief further. I was alone and unloved. Only Xenia remained, murmuring in my ear that my husband was coming. But she, too, was gone. Bereft, I exhausted myself in tears.

Masha entered to say that Gaspari was downstairs. I had no desire to be seen in such a state, but neither would I send away our last friend in the city. "Say that I shall be down presently." I splashed water on my face, then gathered myself together and went downstairs.

He met me with such a look of sorrow that I suspected Masha had already told him our news. But no, he was only mirroring what he found in my face.

"The court has sent away Xenia Grigoryevna?"

"It is not the court's doing, but we must leave nonetheless."

I told him all that had occurred at the courthouse, and what I had written to my father.

"I have some monies put away, and this I would give you. You must allow me to do this, dear friend."

He had been setting aside sums every year so that he might return to Italy. I did not know the amount, but I knew its value.

"I cannot. I have no way to repay you, and it would only forestall what needs to be done."

He looked stricken. An unaccustomed silence fell upon us. He seemed to be making an effort to say something further, but he could find no stories for me now. Xenia entered, wearing Andrei's jacket over her dress. Gaspari stood up from his chair and, bowing, offered it to her.

Taking no notice of his courtesy, she announced to him, "I am going away. This shall be her house."

"Yes. I am greatly saddened to hear it."

She gave him a look of impatience. "This shall be her house," she repeated, and pounded the wall as though to give proof there were no vermin in it.

"Xenia, please. Come and sit." I gestured to Gaspari's chair. "She is distressed by the prospect of our leaving."

"Her distress is shared by all those who will miss you."

"It is well built," Xenia said, "a good marriage portion."

Briefly, I held the hope that in his imperfect understanding of Russian, he might miss her meaning, but I saw in his flushed countenance that he grasped it too well. He fingered his handkerchief and seemed to scan it for flaws.

"Were I"—Gaspari faltered—"were I a man like others, nothing could halt me. But I am not . . . I cannot, how to say . . ." He fluttered his long fingers pitifully as though to conjure the words from the air. "I am not made for marriage."

Xenia dismissed his objection. "None of us is made for marriage. It is made for us."

I tried to put an end to his misery and mine. "Please. You needn't. She doesn't know what she says."

His wretched gaze met mine. "No, she hears the cry of my heart. It does not want you to go. How will I stay on alone in this cold city? They praise my Orfeo and when I sing the part of Procris, they weep. They want to sleep with my Alexander. But I am still the monster. Even when I come to their beds. Who in this cold city hears my heart speak its own words and does not mock me? You, Dasha. If I were whole, I would ask for you so that you might stay."

I felt the floor tip and slide, right itself, and slide in the other direction. I grasped my chair to steady myself and set the room to rights again. I found my tongue.

"Ask."

And so he did. Gaspari made the journey to the country to speak to my father and claim me.

How could I have expected any other reception but that which he got? My father derided him. "So she wishes to marry the jester after all," he said. Apparently, he readily agreed to release me, but he would not release my dowry. Why, he demanded, should he buy a breed horse that had been gelded? And was not his daughter already gaining a house by this marriage? It seems my letter had come to him in the same post with another from Aunt Galya, wherein she made complaints against my character, among them that I was scheming and ungrateful and had taken advantage of her poor daughter's ruined wit to steal her house.

Gaspari bowed and left without protest. He was loath to tell me any of this at the time; when he returned to Petersburg, he said only that we had all we should expect from my father.

"I will ask my brother, Vanya, to speak with him," I said, but Gaspari shook his head.

"A brother will not look on me more kindly."

My humiliation turned to anger. This dowry was rightly mine. Without it, I had nothing to bring to a marriage and was no better than a beggar. With what dignity I could feign, I let Gaspari know that I released him from any obligation.

"Obligation?" He tilted his chin and knitted his brow in the way he had of seeming puzzled or vexed or both. I think it is the habit of someone who must continually question his understanding, for I noticed that he never wore this look when speaking his own tongue.

"It is your father does not want you, Dashenka. My feelings have not changed."

WE WERE WED QUIETLY AND without ceremony. The church would not condone such a marriage, but Gaspari bribed a priest to mutter a few words over us in the vestibule of the church, with Xenia and five musicians from the Italian Company as witnesses.

Upon leaving, Xenia invited the beggars on the steps to share in the wedding supper, and with the priest and this motley company we returned on foot to the house. It was high summer, and the servants had spread blankets in the yard that we might dine *al fresco*, as the Italians say, like peasants in the field at harvesttime.

Toasts were made with both vodka and a sweet liquor that tasted of licorice. One by one, the guests wished us wealth and happiness and long life. *"Per cent'anni,"* the Italians said. For a hundred years. And *"Gor'ko!"* the Russians answered. The vine is bitter, and to make it sweet the bride and groom must kiss.

Gaspari held my chin and put his mouth on mine. His lips were soft and insinuating. I had never been kissed and did not know that a shock of heat can travel between two bodies. I startled and drew back. About me, there were hoots and cheers.

In all this celebration, Xenia had sat apart with the priest. But on hearing the noise, she rose from her seat. "The time has come," she said, and taking me by the hand led me into the house. At the top of the stairs, she turned into her room.

Her bed was dressed in the bridal linens I had stitched more than half my life ago, put away for this night, and then forgotten. Draped across these was a nightgown. I had not seen it for some dozen years, but it was so deeply familiar that my eyes instantly sought the place on the yoke where my mother had sewn a rosette. Next to it was my first imperfect copy—its stitches uneven and lumpy, the linen round it pulled and pricked—and round the yoke the record of my growing skill was visible in each successive flower. I felt again the remembered pressure of the thimble and needle in the tips of my fingers, my furrowed concentration as I had worked this bit of linen. Just as a peasant works his patch of earth—his sweat watering the soil, his prayers tilled into it season after season, and in turn, the soil worked into his brown palms and under his nails—we twine ourselves into a small piece of the world and it becomes us. My old life was suddenly very dear to me.

Xenia pressed a paper into my hand. It was the deed to the house. At the end of the faded document was fresh ink. *In the name of Colonel Andrei Feodorovich Petrov, I bequeath to my cousin, Daria Nikolayevna Pososhkova, this house and all my worldly goods. May she use them to God's glory and in memory of our love.*

Below this, the priest had marked a place for her to sign and added another inscription saying that it was copied and witnessed on this date.

I hesitated, my eyes drifting back to the bed. "But where shall you sleep?"

Was there ever such a dolt? But Xenia did not mind my

ungracious thanks. She began to unlace my dress. "You shall be with your beloved, and I with mine." She helped me to remove my undergarments until I was naked and shivering, though the night was warm. Below the open window, the Italians had begun to serenade. Their high voices drifted up and snared in the limbs of the plane tree and fluttered its leaves so that they sparked with the last lights of the evening sun.

She slipped the gown over my head, and my arms into the sleeves, and the moment was upon us. The feeling rose up in me that I was departing on a long journey from which I should not return. Like all travelers, I wished to sit with her in silence for a time before I set out, but I could not give voice to this and so, as she started to leave, I impulsively threw my arms round her and clung as though we were about to be parted forever. She stroked my hair, and after a time loosened herself from my grasp. "He is waiting." And with this, she closed the door behind her and left me alone.

I do not know how long I remained there before Gaspari knocked. It must have surprised him to enter and find such an immodest and eager-seeming bride standing just on the far side of the door.

"You are not in bed." He, too, was dressed in a nightgown, and though this was unremarkable given the circumstances, I had not anticipated it. Transfixed, I stared at the curve of his breasts beneath the thin linen. In the baths, I had seen the bodies of men and of women, but I had never seen this.

He went to the window and closed it, muting the sounds

of music. Then he pulled fast the drapery and, blessedly, dissolved from view. I allowed myself to be led to the bed and lifted up onto it. In the dark, I heard his breathing and felt his hand at my waist, very gentle.

My recollection of what followed has the quality of a fever dream in which the most astonishing happenings—such that could scarcely be imagined by the waking self—are met by the dreamer without question. My body, suddenly unfamiliar to me, was revealed to be a map that could be read by touch. His hands, soft as a woman's, found those places where the soul lay just beneath the surface, like coals banked in a white ash of skin. His tongue worked in more secret places, speaking a hitherto unsuspected language. With quiet insistence, he coaxed from me a wild fluency. I writhed and cried and burbled gibberish and was by all outward and inward signs overtaken by a kind of lunacy from which I emerged spent and badly shaken. I began to weep. It frightened me how thin is the membrane that separates us from madness. I thought of Xenia.

"Did you not enjoy it?"

I did not know how to answer. "I thought I should die."

"It is called the little death."

I was hotly ashamed, but I had to know. "Is this what others do?"

"Most take their pleasure more directly. What they say, a means? To get children? But I was not created to get, only to give. However poor, it is my gift to please." For all the seeming modesty of his words, there was pride in his voice.

"But if it gives you no pleasure—"

"No, no, it makes me very happy." He found my hand. "You are like figs, Dashenka."

DID YOU NOT ENJOY IT? Xenia had asked this same question of me several years earlier. I had accompanied her and Andrei to Grand Duchess Catherine's summer palace, Oranienbaum. As a winter entertainment for Catherine's court, an immense sliding hill had been constructed of timbered frames in the shape of an upended bow and bricked with polished ice so that one might slide down one slope and then up the facing side. It was smaller than the famed Flying Mountain that is there now, but more treacherous, for there was no track to hold the sledge to its course, nothing to prevent it from spilling over the edge.

At Xenia's urging, we mounted the steps to the top. From this vantage could be seen the entire breadth of the park, the palace in the distance and, gleaming dully like a river, a long ribbon of ice falling away from the platform where we stood. Donkeys and serfs working with ropes were hauling a small sledge back upstream. It resembled a coffin fit with runners. They heaved it up onto the platform, and then waited on us with horrible expectancy.

Together with the driver, we were wedged into this conveyance, Xenia in front and I behind her. Then we were pushed to the lip of the precipice—and over. The sledge careened down the steep incline, ice rushing towards us and all else blurred by terrifying speed. I buried my eyes in the only solid thing, Xenia's back. She was screaming. I felt the weightless velocity of our descent in my liquefied bones.

Then, with a nauseating heave, we reversed course and began to slide backwards, falling and falling and falling. At
long last, the sledge began to slow, and finally it came to
a rest. We emerged, miraculously unharmed. Xenia was
laughing, breathless and eager to ride again.

"It is like flying!" she said, and was puzzled that I did
not share her euphoria.

THE MORNING FOLLOWING THE WEDDING, Xenia was gone
from the house. I thought nothing of this, but when she did
not return by late afternoon I sent Grishka to the church to
fetch her. He returned and reported that she had not been
seen there. I sent him directly back out to look for her at
Andrei's grave. So narrow were her habits that I could not
conceive of any other destination, but even before he returned, a part of me knew she had gone much farther.

I found myself standing outside Andrei's room. Since his
death, the door had remained closed, but that morning it
stood ajar. I entered. In the faded heat of the midsummer
evening, the room was close. Everything in it was silted
with a fine sheath of dust, but otherwise it seemed much as
it had been while he was alive. Because he slept in Xenia's
room, it was not furnished with a bed but only a dressing
table, a boot chair and commode, a standing mirror, and
other such accoutrements as are necessary to a gentleman's
dressing room. His wig was now gone from its stand, and
there were clean shapes on the dressing table where formerly
there had been jars of pomade and powder and whatnot. She
had given some of his things away, yet by comparison to the

looted appearance of the rest of the house the room seemed overstuffed with possessions.

For this reason, perhaps, it was some moments before I saw Xenia's black mourning dress, her last remaining garment, discarded on the floor of the empty armoire. When I picked it up, something fell from its folds: the delicate cross and chain she had worn round her neck since infancy. Apprehension knifed through me.

Still, I had only a foreboding and nothing material to pin it to. In the weeks that followed, I returned to the church and to Smolenskoye cemetery again and again, thinking I might find her or some sign that she had been there. I sought her out in increasingly unlikely quarters of the city as well, asking at churches and taverns and wherever people were congregated if any had seen a woman of about my years but more comely and answering to the name Xenia Grigoryevna. That by all appearances she had left the house unclothed would suggest that someone should have remembered seeing her, but it was as though she had been removed from the earth and no trace left behind.

We went to the authorities, but they were uniformly uninterested—women go missing all the time, murdered or escaped from husbands or fathers or masters. As Xenia belonged to no one, no husband or father or master, she might go where she pleased and they had no cause to find her and bring her back. Yes, said one uncurious officer, it was less common for a woman to leave behind even her clothing. But then again, he added, the rivers are full of madwomen.

When it was spoken aloud, my foreboding instantly assumed material form. I recalled the terms of her parting from me on my wedding night. "You shall be with your beloved, and I with mine." How had I missed the portent in these words when she said them? Why would she give me her house except that she saw no further need of it herself? Why had I not questioned this gift?

The answer came to me that I had not questioned it because I had need of a house.

After this, I could not cross a bridge without my gaze drifting down to the water and seeking there her countenance, wavering dim and green in the depths. What I found was only my own reflection on the surface. I contemplated Lake Svetloyar and the pilgrims who had gone there and disappeared.

At the end of a fortnight, Gaspari was compelled to return to the Italian Company, which was still in summer residence with the court at Tsarskoye Selo. I could not bring myself to desert the city. "If she were to return . . ." I explained. He agreed, though I saw in his face that it was only out of kindness and an unwillingness to destroy what hope I had.

In truth, this hope was small and unsteady. Strung between unsettled expectation and despair, on some days I prayed fervently that God might bring her back to me and at other times I asked only for her bones that I might lay my grief to rest alongside them. Later still, my supplications were even more faltering and exhausted. Give me only this, I prayed, the reassurance of your presence. But my thoughts floated outwards and came back thin as an echo. I continued to look for her on the church steps, but she was never there, and I went less often. At some moment unmarked by me, the low flame of my faith guttered and went out.

## CHAPTER TWELVE

The musici were notorious for being temperamental—it was widely held that the sacrifice of their manhood unbalanced their humors—and Gaspari's reputation in the court was no different. Stories of his unrestrained behavior circulated through the court: that he had insisted on being reseated above the salt at a supper and then left anyway, that he had ripped up a score because he did not like the composition, that he canceled performances for no better reason than that he objected to the weather. Of course, one cannot depend upon wags for the truth if it can be improved by exaggeration and falsehoods. In truth, the thin blood of Italians is unsuited to our climate, and Gaspari suffered most grievously in the winter. He was often wracked with terrible chills and coughs, and if he did not perform, it was because of this. And while it is true that he once called Alexi Bestuzhev-Ryumin a horse's ass and refused to sing a note unless the Grand Chancellor was first removed from the building, it was not reported that the Grand Chancellor had earlier insulted him very grievously or that the whole matter came to nothing once it was discovered that there had been a misunderstanding and the Grand Chancellor was not, after all, present at the opera house that evening.

I doubt the world would have credited how unassuming a man Gaspari was within our walls and how generous to his friends, but he did nothing to help his own cause. Perceiving that most persons found him strange and repellent, he moved through society with a haughty air, stiffening at whispers and sensitive to imagined slights. And if any person had the temerity to talk while he sang or to applaud tepidly afterwards, that person was forever his enemy. Even fawning admiration, though he craved it, might arouse in him suspicions that he was being mocked, and he would then retaliate with a barbed wit.

As the cognoscenti prize most what is most rare and delicate, they tolerated what they deemed this capriciousness and even encouraged it. They wanted monsters, and so they had them.

In the year that followed Xenia's disappearance, Araja announced that he would revive his *Alessandro nell'Indie*, the opera that had first brought Gaspari to the attention of Petersburg. With the singer Carestini gone to London, Gaspari anticipated taking the *primo uomo* role of the Indian King Poro who battled with Alexander the Great for the love of his Indian Queen, Cleofide.

Gaspari was violently offended, then, to learn that Araja had awarded the role instead to Lorenzo Saletti for his return to the Russian court. "It is the faithful dog is kicked," Gaspari said.

He took up his old part, that of Alexander, but returned from rehearsal the first day frothing with bitterness towards Saletti, who was, he claimed, so past his vigor that his listeners must envy the deaf. "Squeak, squeak, squeak! I cannot bear it! I cannot pretend to a noble contest with this fat, old mouse. I should be chasing him about the stage with the broom!"

He grew increasingly distressed with each rehearsal. It physically pained Gaspari to hear a sour note, and though he did his best to shield himself from the assaults by covering his ears while Saletti sang, it was more than he could endure. He broke down into weeping one night, and I feared he would not last until the evening of the first performance.

It was my habit to watch his performances from the wings, where I could not be seen. Sitting in the house meant suffering the many eyes that peered at me from behind fans, the trail of titters that attended my coming or going. "The musico's wife," they would whisper, and I knew they were thinking of what we did in our bed.

And so, on the first evening, after I had helped Gaspari with his dressing, I tucked myself behind a bit of scenery, where I should be out of the way.

Saletti took the stage in his gold turban and striped robes, assumed a pose, and without yet singing a note brought the audience to a cheer. When he had drunk his fill of it, he began to sing. He was indeed past his strength, though not so terrible as my husband had portrayed him. I looked over to Gaspari, who stood in the shadow of the proscenium awaiting his own entrance. His painted features twisted at each wavering note, and I worried that he might turn and leave the theatre. But as I watched, he closed his eyes and shook loose his long limbs.

As Saletti scaled the last treacherous note of his aria, Gaspari strutted onto the stage, swishing his purple robe in glorious arcs of color, and planted himself in the center of the footlights. He did not wait even a beat after Saletti's last note before he began to sing himself, and thus he deprived the older musico of any applause. For the length of the opera, Gaspari greatly embellished his part, departing from the score to weave in filigrees of trilling and florid ornamentation. The battle between Alexander and the Indian King for the love of Cleofide was a contest also between the two musici, and it was one that Saletti could not win. To hear them singing together was to see history reenacted and to understand how Alexander had so thoroughly vanquished and humiliated India.

At the end of the second act, Gaspari finished his final aria with an exquisite *messa di voce*, sustaining a single note, letting it swell and then fade almost to nothing before it rose again like a phoenix. The audience was stirred to its feet and shouted its bravos. Rather than exiting, Gaspari remained near the lip of the stage as Saletti sang, that he might relish the unflattering comparisons being made in the house.

This triumph did not appease Gaspari's pricked vanity. He talked more frequently of quitting Russia—moving to Italy or even to Paris, where the climate was more temperate and he might be better appreciated—but he was too much rewarded in the employ of Her Imperial Majesty to give it up as yet for uncertain prospects. And so we continued to live a quiet life in the shadow of the court.

There was little left in the house to remind me of Xenia. So many of the furnishings had been sold or given away, and the repetitive tasks of domesticity—the sweeping and cleaning and polishing—gradually erased her signature from what remained. I did not forget her, but the sharp pain of her loss softened and became like a swollen joint or weakened back. One accommodates the ache, and it becomes a part of you.

Because I could have no expectation of children, I had schooled myself not to want them, having learnt from Xenia the peril of unchecked longing. I managed the household well and was attentive to my husband's particular needs, keeping the stove fueled at night in the worst of winter and tucking cooked stones wrapped in flannel round his feet. When in spite of this he took ill, I stayed at his bedside and fed him strong broths. I also learnt to prepare dishes of his birthplace and even taught myself some few phrases of Italian that he might feel himself more at home here. As Xenia had for Andrei, I brought him warm kvas with honey and herbs for his throat. However, what had been at the heart of that little gesture—a passionate and unreserved love—I could not give. Perhaps I was unwilling to fall again into the abyss that had so frightened me on the first night of our marriage. I think I held myself a little apart.

Did he sense any shortcoming in my heart? I do not know. I think we were happy enough.

•    •    •

SEASON FOLLOWED SEASON, EACH ALIKE except for the small changes that every year brings—a new opera or a new way to wear a wig, shifts in alliances between person and person or country and country—diversions that fill our days with seeming import but are then displaced by whatever newer thing follows. At some point during this time, the Empress engaged the architect Rastrelli to design a splendid new masonry palace on the site of the old Winter Palace. For this work, thousands of laborers were absorbed into the city and took up residence in huts near the site. They labored there for years, the enormous structure rising by such slow increments as to seem unchanging, as though it had always been there in its unfinished state.

The war begun against Prussia in 1756 also rumbled on ceaselessly, a tidal ebb and flow of battle lines that washed over the whole of Europe but was present to me only in the person of my brother, Vanya. Cut off by my family, I had no news of him until his death at Züllichau, which I learnt of when the rolls were published in the papers. In a dull fog, I was on the point of traveling to the country to console my parents, but Gaspari prevented it. "There is nothing there for you, Dashenka," he said. "They do not love you. I am all your family now." After that, I did not take an interest in the war again until I was forced to by circumstances that I will relate.

On Christmas Day of 1761, the tolling of the bells brought news of the death of Her Imperial Majesty. I re-member feeling no shock. She was old—or so it seemed then, though it occurs to me that she was younger by several years than I am now—and she had been ill for so long, her death predicted so repeatedly that when it arrived it felt like the exhalation of a long-held breath.

No one of our acquaintance was happy at the prospect of her nephew, Grand Duke Peter, taking the throne, but I did not anticipate how this would change our lives or with what suddenness. Within two days of her death, the new Emperor dismissed the Italian Company from the service of the court. Only a fortnight before, Elizabeth had issued a decree to recruit more actors and musicians for the troupe. Now he ordered the theatre shuttered, with all its stock of scenery, effects, machinery, and costumes left inside to molder. Peter moved himself into the dead Empress's still-unfinished palace and set about to wipe clean from memory all the graces of her reign.

Gaspari was then suffering the annual toll that our winters took on him, a perpetual weariness from always being cold, but this seeming reversal of his fortunes had a tonic effect. His spirits rose at the news and for this reason: there was nothing to keep us here any longer. He might now return to Italy. He had succeeded in putting by more than enough funds to keep us in comfort until he found a position. We might go first to the village where he had been born. He happily anticipated showing it to me—the terraced hills with their low stone walls, the lion's head over the door of his mother's house—and, in turn, showing me to his relations. These were, by his account, most all of the village.

I made an effort to share his joy, but he knew me too well not to feel the thinness of my enthusiasm. "I know what I ask, Dasha . . . but I will die if I stay here." And then he tried to cheer me with this: so much of Petersburg, the palaces and canals and bridges, were but poor copies of what I should find in Italy. "And everything looks more happy there," he added, "because it is where it belongs." He wrote to his mother with the news that he was coming home and bringing with him his Russian wife.

The war had made private travel treacherous, and the route to Italy passed through Prussia, where we could not go. However, in his eagerness to quit Russia, Gaspari found a means. An envoy to the ministry at Leipzig had been appointed to announce His Majesty's accession to the throne and would leave on this mission shortly. Gaspari approached Countess Stroganova, who was a devoted follower of the new Emperor, and secured from her the favor of our being attached to Prince Bezborodko's travel party.

I gathered together the household and said that I wished to free them to settle their own futures. If they had a place to go, I would see to their papers; if not, they might serve my aunt Galina Stepanovna. With many tears, we began to pack our belongings that we should be ready to leave within the week. Passports were arranged for Gaspari and me, and because I could not bring myself to sell it, the house was put with an agent to let.

Christ instructed his disciples not to lay up their treasure on earth but in Heaven. For where your treasure is, there shall your heart be also. But the heart stubbornly attaches itself to familiar places and things and would rather have these, no matter how humble, than to exchange them for the promise of what is glorious but unknown. That Italy's skies would be as yellow as Paradise did not console me; I preferred the granite shadows of this most bleak and most beautiful city. Even the history of my sadness here was dear to me.

On the day before we were to set out, I made to bid our dear Empress good-bye and joined the thousands of mourners lined up outside the old wooden palace where she lay in state. Though she had been his benefactress, Gaspari could not risk his health by lingering out of doors, but he urged me to go and to say his prayers for him. I was glad for the time to be alone with my thoughts; the grave sky and the mournful aspect of the crowd were well tuned to my mood.

I waited several hours to gain entrance to the death chamber, standing behind two women whom I took by their conversation to be soldiers' wives. Reflecting that where I was going I should not hear my native tongue, I sucked in the earthy sounds of it. They began talking of the rumor that our new Emperor Peter would suspend hostilities against his beloved Frederick, the Emperor of Prussia.

"No, surely not," said one, "not with victory so close."

The other raised her brow meaningfully. "They say he speaks German with his advisors."

My thoughts wandered elsewhere until I heard one of the women speak a familiar name. Andrei Feodorovich. "She foretold this, you know," the woman continued to her companion. "I saw her outside the church. She was tearing at her clothes and crying out to passersby to go home and bake blinis."

Hope startled awake in me, coursing into my veins as sudden and violent as a spring river.

"For a funeral supper?" the one woman asked.

The other nodded gravely. "What else would you make of it? And two days later, Her Majesty was dead."

"Excuse me." I interrupted their talk. "Who is it you are speaking of?"

"The Empress," she answered.

"Yes, yes, but you heard someone foretell her death?"

The woman nodded.

"Whereabouts was this church?"

The woman's features stiffened at my abruptness. "In St. Matthias parish," she said, and then turned back to her friend.

"Please," I implored. She eyed me once more, warily. "Just answer me this. Was the person's name Xenia Grigoryevna?"

"No."

In spite of this, I left my place in the line and hired a droshky to take me straightaway to the church in St. Matthias.

We crossed the river and drove until we came to a shabby neighborhood within this poorest of boroughs. Tumbledown wooden houses, shops, and huts were crowded together like broken teeth, seeming to be kept upright only by their leaning against one another. The unpaved streets were a quagmire, with pigs and starving dogs rooting about in the filth. The air was pestilential, and I kept my hand-kerchief over my face to blunt the stench. When we came upon the church, I leapt down from the droshky and hastily made my way to its steps.

I found no dearth of the afflicted there, but Xenia was not among them, nor did anyone know her name.

The repeated denials, and the sights and smells of this benighted place wore down my resolve and allowed a small, sensible voice within me to be heard. *Why have you come here? The woman said that it was not Xenia. And there are many in the world by the name of Andrei Feodorovich. Would you be like her, seeking meaning in every coincidence?*

*Go with your husband to Italy. Everything is dead for you here.*

## CHAPTER THIRTEEN

I looked out the carriage window as we passed through the gate of the city and were swallowed into the forest. Later, the terrain changed to wintry swamp and meadows, with snow spread like linen over the sleeping earth. Except for a few feathery stands of birch, the panorama, earth to sky, was unbroken and peaceful. How does the soil rest, I wondered, where it is always warm and never dormant? But beside my misgivings was also curiosity. I had conjured pictures of a place that was like Petersburg in summer, but covered in vines, and I had peopled it with the Italians at court. The Italy of my imagination was a land of dark-eyed women and musici.

Gaspari kept up a steady conversation with an aide to the Prince, with whom we shared the carriage. I can only guess at what this aide must have thought privately of us, the Italian musico and his Russian wife, but when traveling one must put aside the scruples that govern one's choice of company in the city, and Nikolai Yakovlevich was a young man of lenient character, not above being entertained by

Gaspari. As I have mentioned, my husband was an excellent gossip, and our departure from Petersburg had freed him of any remaining constraints on his tongue. He felt no need for discretion, for he intended never to return there. His mood was expansive and, fueled by frequent draughts of vodka to keep off the cold, he amused himself and the young man with his appraisals of Petersburg's fools and fops. When we stopped at an inn for the night, he ordered warm kvas and invited Nikolai Yakovlevich to sit by the stove with him that they might continue their talk.

"This I will say——" He rubbed life back into his hands. "She was strong as a man. No other country could a woman rule. I think it is these winters. It makes the woman . . . what is the word I want?"

Nikolai Yakovlevich smiled genially but was too politic to supply any word.

"Bold," Gaspari pronounced. "That is it. These Russian woman is like new steel that is put in cold water to harden." He gauged the young man's expression and smiled ruefully. "I do not offend by this? Good. I admire. Myself, I was not made for this cold. I am like the little songbird that forget to fly away when the summer ends."

At Novgorod, we left the road I knew and turned west to the sea. The journey from here to Riga is three long days at a gallop but five at the Prince's more leisured pace, for he disliked being woken early. When poor horses were all that could be had at a post station, we added yet another day.

By the fourth, Gaspari's spirits had subdued. He grew listless and quiet. Following Nikolai Yakovlevich's glance out the window, he said, "White and white and then more white. Not a pretty village even to relieve the—" He coughed into his handkerchief. "*Pardonnez-moi*, to relieve the dullness. If you will travel on to Italy with us, my friend, you shall see such pretty villages."

On the fifth day, Gaspari gave off talking entirely and huddled quietly under a fur lap robe, jounced out of a sluggish doze every so often by a rough patch of road or a fit of coughing. By the time we arrived in Riga, he was unmistakably ill.

We were to be guests there of the Governor General, in a castle which housed the local administration. It was an ancient, formidable hulk seemingly little changed in centuries. The Governor greeted the Prince and his entourage and escorted us into a gray hall that was more frigid than the out-of-doors. Here he made such ceremony of his welcome that Gaspari, unwrapped from his travel robes, began to shiver and look pale. I thought he might faint and was obliged to ask that he be shown directly to a room.

In spite of its furnishings, the room where he was taken had the appearance of a dungeon. Its dank stone walls were ill-concealed by tapestries and breathed a chill that was not dispelled by the stove in the corner. There was no good in putting him to bed there, so I entreated one of the servants to see that the banya be heated and when this was done took him there that he might sweat out the ill humors. He stayed in the bath almost all of the night and into the next day.

The Prince was to dine that evening with the Governor

General, and it had been expected that Gaspari would sing. Much had been made of this, for though the Governor kept a serf orchestra, there was little variety to his entertainments. But when Nikolai Yakovlevich came to inquire after Gaspari, I had to tell him there was no question of it—though my husband's color was somewhat better, his lungs were still so wet that he had only been able to sleep by being propped upright. In truth, I doubted that he should be well enough to travel the next day.

Nikolai Yakovlevich studied his hands, his mouth twisting thoughtfully. "I regret that the Prince's chief concern must be the mission entrusted to him."

His meaning broke over me like a sudden sweat. The Prince would not be inclined to delay his departure on account of an entertainer, more particularly one who could no longer entertain. Nor could we follow at a later time across the Prussian border, not without the diplomatic protection afforded by the crown. If Gaspari could not travel tomorrow, our only recourse would be to remain in Riga until he was recovered and then return to Petersburg.

"Perhaps he will be more rested by morning," I said.

"We must pin our hopes to that."

Gaspari would not hear of either staying or turning back. Feeble as he was, he insisted that he should be better on the morrow. "If I must sing for my supper tonight, I will do this also." He rose and made to dress.

Never before had I seen him risk his voice for any cause. Not even Her Imperial Majesty could command a performance from him if he was sick. Yet, had he been able to dress unassisted, I do not think I could have dissuaded him from his rash course.

As it was, he was overtaken by a fit of coughing before he had gotten further than his stockings and garters. I helped him back into his bed.

"If you would travel, you will need all your rest."

The next day, we continued on, through Courland and into Lithuania. His condition worsened throughout the day such that by the time we arrived in the evening at an inn, he was shaking with fever and had need to be lifted from the carriage and borne inside. A healer from the nearby village was sent for.

Perhaps the old woman was told something of her patient by the innkeeper's wife, who brought her to the door. Or perhaps it was only a mistrust of all foreigners that caused her to peer in at Gaspari with such dourness. Whatever the cause, she would not cross the threshold of his room without first seeing the contents of my purse. After tucking the coins into her apron, she unpacked her glass cups and put them on the stove to heat.

"Are we in Prussia?" Gaspari whispered. His eyes were glazed.

"Very close."

"How many days to Leipzig?"

"I do not know."

He nodded and his eyes closed again.

The healer came to the bedside with a cup. When she turned back the coverlet and opened Gaspari's nightshirt to put it on his chest, she started back at the sight of his bosom, and the cup dropped from her hand and shattered. She cried out something in German.

"He is a musico," I said helplessly. I did not know the German word but doubted it would mean anything to her had I known it. "Look," I said, and reached down to Gaspari's throat and touched the cross round his neck. "Tell her," I said to the mistress, "he was made like this for God's glory." The two women exchanged rapid, guttural words before the mistress turned back to me and shook her head.

"He is sick," I pleaded, and I tried to offer more coins to the old woman, but she backed away from me as if I were a demon, hastily gathered up her paraphernalia, and left.

I sat down on the edge of the bed and rested my hand on his brow. It was hot and dry. A tear leaked from the corner of one of his closed eyes and trickled onto the pillow.

I went from the room and found the mistress in the passage, returning from having let the old woman out. I asked her for the makings of a plaster. "At the least, you can spare my husband some flour and mustard and a rag." I was trembling with fury. "Oh, and a broom to sweep up the glass. I will not trouble you to sweep it yourself." She looked on me with a closed and wary expression and shook her head.

"Not even this?" I was beside myself.

"More slow, please," she said in halting Russian.

"A broom," I repeated, and made the motions of sweeping. She nodded energetically and quite nearly ran down the passage, returning shortly with what I had asked for. When I nodded and held out my hand for it, she wagged her forefinger, and said something in German.

I followed her back to the room, and as she swept, I tried to think how my paltry words of German might be bent to acquire a plaster.

The Empress Catherine has since made it fashionable to play at dumb charades—my grandchildren love the game—but I doubt even the most skilled player could puzzle out such a challenge. I patted and rubbed my chest and then pointed to Gaspari. She nodded and lifted up her own bosom as if to say, yes, we all three shared this attribute in common. I shook my head and repeated my gestures, first miming scooping up paste into my hand, but fixed as she was on Gaspari's deformity we made no headway. I asked her if there was someone who spoke Russian. She fetched the innkeeper, I found Nikolai Yakovlevich, and we four at last blundered our way to understanding, whereupon she took me to the larder and gave me what was needed. I returned to my husband.

"I am putting this on your chest, *cuoricino mio.*"

Gaspari's eyes were closed, and he was past the effort of answering, but he nodded.

"It will be warm."

I spread the rag over the delicate skin of his chest and then, dipping my fingers into the brown paste, gently smoothed it onto him. When I was finished, I wiped the paste from my hands and continued to smooth out the skin on his brow and temples. I knew each blemish, each line, the blue thread that ran under the skin on his temple, the mole on the lobe of his ear. Each in its familiarity was infinitely dear to me, and I tried to make him feel this through my touch. I ran my fingers down the long slope of his neck to the clavicle, and they came to rest in the hollow of his throat where an Adam's apple would be on another man. His heart pulsed into my fingers. Memorize this, I thought.

His eyes opened and he reached up to grasp my hand. "I hoped . . ." he began. His voice was low and clotted. " . . . To see Italy again."

"I know, dearest. We shall go when you are well again. Nikolai Yakovlevich has said we might try again this summer. He thinks we shall have peace by then."

"You won't leave me here?"

"Leave you? No. I would never leave you."

He was quiet for a moment. With my free hand, I smoothed his hair, felt his scalp.

"But you will go back to Russia," he said, and then waited for me to understand his meaning. "So I shall return there, too."

I OBSERVED THE DEPARTURE OF the Prince and his entourage from the inn the next day, watching their carriages until they were only a line of black specks on the snow, listening to the last faint sound of harness bells, and then not even that. My German hosts spoke freely between themselves as though I were not there, and this sense of being a spectator to my own life was increased by my understanding nothing of what was said. By the quickness with which they averted their eyes when I looked, I suspected they were discussing my circumstances. This was affirmed by the mistress coming to me and, still speaking in German but more slowly, gesturing to the dining room and making the motion of putting fork to mouth. Certainly, it is a universal instinct to feed those who are troubled. I had no appetite, but courtesy forbade my declining, and so I sat at table with them and obligingly spooned food into my mouth. The husband and wife looked on with approval, and the serving girl watched from the corner.

*"Sehr gut,"* I said, though in truth I might have been gumming rubber and paste. *"Danke."* They urged more on me, but their eyes were so full of sympathy that my throat closed up and I could not swallow any more. After this, I stayed in Gaspari's room. A coach brought new guests to the inn; I heard the muted sounds of voices and of snow being knocked from boots.

Between the mistress and her servant girl, a steady rotation of this and that was brought to the door. Gaspari's linens were changed and fresh plasters applied, the wicks trimmed, and the stove banked or fed. Upon leaving, they removed the untouched plates of food. For long hours, there was nothing left for me to do but wipe Gaspari's brow and listen to the terrible bellows of his breath.

I remember thinking to myself, you are watching your husband die, and in a matter of hours, at most a day or two, he will be gone from this earth. I tested the assertion in my mind, and it seemed both unreal and irrefutable. Tears rose up and puddled in my eyes, but they were like drops leaking through a chink in a dam and gave no relief.

When the moment of his death did come, there was nothing to mark it but a cessation of breath and then a profound stillness. He was there and then, quite visibly, he was not. I marveled at this. Absent the spirit and the promise of heaven in his voice, what remained was so plainly a mask.

# The Holy Fool of
# Petersburg

## CHAPTER FOURTEEN

The horrible days of his death and the slow journey back to Petersburg with his coffin strapped to the rear of the public coach—I recall this with more grief than I felt at the time. I was cloaked in numbness.

For one whose voice had inspired fervent admiration, Gaspari had left behind in Russia hardly enough mourners to bear his coffin to its resting place. His tailor and three stranded members of the Italian Company put him in unconsecrated ground. As his coffin was lowered, I remember worrying that come winter the ground would be too cold for him, much colder than if he had been in Italy.

I brought Masha back—I was obliged to buy her from Nadya, though I had not sold her—and I attempted to take up my old life, remaking my routines round the absence at their center. A stranger to myself, I kneaded bread enough for a larger household. I forgot and then remembered a dozen times in a day that there was no cause now for the glass of kvas or the plate of anchovies, no need to build the fire so hot.

During this same time, Catherine seized the throne from her husband, the new Emperor, by riding into Petersburg at the head of the Imperial Guards. Within days, Peter the Third was dead by mysterious hands. These momentous happenings were like thunder heard at a great distance: they did not touch me. I slept at odd hours and then was wakeful through the night. What came to me in these hours were all my sins of omission, those small tendernesses I might have shown Gaspari while he still lived, and words I might have said to ease his passage into the hereafter. *Dear friend,* I might have said—as I have said a hundred times since—*you were a great gift to me.*

These regrets haunted me even into the day. I attempted to escape them through working, and when this failed I fled the house to distance myself from its associations. Going out to take the air, I would later find myself in some unfamiliar place, and with no memory of how I had come there.

I had no cause to return to St. Matthias parish. But I rose early one morning after another night of broken sleep, hired a droshky, and directed the driver to take me across the river. On the steps of the church there, I distributed coins to the poor. If I had hoped by this to gain some relief, I did not; the squalor of the place and the desperate circumstances of the people only increased my despondency. I could not bear even to stay for the service. Thinking only how to get away quickly, I gave up protecting my skirt against the foulness in the street and set off in search of another droshky to take me home. A short distance from the church, I found the same one I had dismissed, stopped before a tavern. The driver was not about, but thinking he would return momentarily I got in it to wait.

There was such a menagerie in the street, both man and beast, that I took no special notice of a fool approaching the droshky, thin and shabbily dressed and talking to the air—there are many such creatures in Petersburg, and they are generally harmless and pitiable souls. He stopped and fastened his attention on the horse, then extracted a parsnip from the jacket of his pocket. The horse nickered and bobbed at its bridle, and the fool, bobbing his head in response, began to sing as it fed from his hand.

It was his tune that snagged my attention.

*"This poor sinner only prays"*—the fool nuzzled the nose of the horse with his own as he sang—*"to be kissed to Paradise."*

All at once and with a shock, I knew.

EVEN HAD SHE NOT BEEN dressed as a man, I might not have recognized Xenia except by the song. She was filthy, her hair matted as felt, and her garments stained and worn to threads.

Steadying myself, I came down from the droshky and approached her with the quiet demeanor one would use to tame a wild bird. "Xenia?"

Her gaze turned at my voice.

"It is Dasha," I said.

"Are you looking for Xenia?" she asked. There was such a sweetness in her face—it is beyond my poor powers to describe—as if all of life's harshness had been wiped clean from it, leaving her soft and unscarred.

I nodded. "I looked everywhere. We thought you had . . ." In spite of my intent, my voice broke.

The horse was nudging her pocket. "He could use another."

"Where did you go, darling?" I asked.

"Do you have one?"

"A parsnip?"

"Any vegetable will do. He is not particular."

"No." I asked her again where she had gone.

She cocked her head. "I am here. This is all of me."

Never mind for now, I thought. I held fast to this: she had returned to me. For the moment, it was more than enough. I took both her hands in mine, and she did not resist this.

"Let us go home," I said.

She was content to get into the droshky, but for the length of our journey Xenia said nothing. Her attention was entirely taken up by the passing scenes, and she seemed equally pleased by all prospects. As we approached the house, I expected some change in her aspect, but there was none. The driver stopped before our door.

"Do you not remember your house?" I asked.

"I do not have one of these," she answered cheerfully.

"Of course you do. This is your home."

The driver would take no fare. "Not for her," he demurred. I wondered briefly at this, but it was one with the strangeness of the morning.

Masha opened the front door. Upon seeing Xenia, she

knew her instantly and burst into tears and kissed her shoulders. Xenia received these affections and allowed herself to be led inside.

"We shall have tea, but would you like to bathe first?" I asked.

"Would you like me to?"

Truth be told, her stink was bad, but I answered that I was thinking only of her comfort.

She laughed brightly. "My comfort is not your concern. Or mine either." She was perfectly amenable to bathing if it would please me; I confessed that it would please me very much.

She stained the water brown as a flood stream. When at last she was clean, she looked to put on her breeches again.

"I have a dress for you." I offered one of mine, but she shook her head and would not take it.

"It is black."

"Yes. I am a widow now, too."

"I wear red and green, you know."

I could make nothing of this, but as she was immoveable on this point I was compelled to retrieve her garments, which Masha was on the point of burning.

"She wants them back," I said.

Masha crossed herself. "They are *his*," she said, and began to weep again.

The jacket and breeches were Andrei's old military uniform, the same that had been altered so many years before that Xenia might wear them to the metamorphoses ball. The green jacket was scarcely more than a rag now and the breeches darkened with filth to the color of dried blood.

"They should be burned," Masha said.

"I think we shall have to humor her for the present. Here now—" I handed her my handkerchief. "Come inside and make us tea."

Tea is not the extravagance now that it was then. When Gaspari was still alive, I had brewed it by the thimbleful to cure his cough, and a little remained. I instructed Masha to put the last of it in the pot.

When I returned the clothes to Xenia, I suggested that I might have others of the same cut and color made for her. She answered just as she had to the bath: if it would please me she was amenable.

After she had dressed, we went into the drawing room. Masha brought in a tray with the tea things, a fat wedge of mutton pie, and a raisin cake. When she saw Xenia, her eyes filled again and the glasses tinkled unsteadily on the tray.

I motioned her to set it down. "I will pour."

Masha bowed and, wiping at her eyes with the corner of her apron, fled the room. Xenia's eyes, alert as a deer's, followed her.

"It has been a long time," I explained, "and she has missed you. Meat or sweet? Xenia?"

Her attention remained on the doorway. I put the pie on a plate.

"Tea?" I did not wait on an answer but poured some into a glass and stirred in two spoons of honey. I invited her to sit and she did, though on the floor beside the chair rather than on the chair itself. I handed her the glass, cautioning her as I did to be mindful that it was hot. Obediently, she set it down on the floor beside her. I poured another glass.

"You are here," I said. I could not entirely absorb the fact of her presence. It is usual when two dear friends have been parted for many years to slake their thirst for one another's company with talk, but Xenia seemed not to feel the need. "I thought you were drowned."

Did she nod? I cannot remember, but I had the distinct impression that she knew this already, though she did not say so and it makes no sense that she would.

"I, too, have missed you," I said. "Terribly."

Though she did not utter a word, her placid gaze was so sympathetic that I talked for us both. I poured out all that had passed in her absence, my life with Gaspari, our intent to go to Italy, and how he had died. Nothing I said surprised her; she only nodded, but with such pure and simple understanding that I unburdened myself further.

"I failed to love him," I said.

This thought had tormented me, a sliver buried in the flesh, but when I spoke it aloud, I saw it was untrue.

"No, I loved him. But I failed to know it."

My love for Gaspari had been there all along, for how many years, so quiet that I had been no more aware of it than the pulse of my own blood. Only when he was gone did I feel it, and then as a terrible, aching absence.

"I opened myself so narrowly." As I said this, tears formed. "And now he is gone, I am hollowed out, *opustoshyonnaya*, and can feel nothing."

She smiled at me with exquisite gentleness.

"In nothing, we have all we need. This emptiness is sweet."

How could she say that she had all she needed? My dear cousin had been deprived of everything that was life to her: her child and her husband and finally her reason. She had not even a kopek to her name. And perhaps not even her name, I thought, recalling that when I found her she had referred to herself in the third person. There could be nothing sweet in this.

She lifted her glass and drained the cold tea in a single, long swallow. "The vessel must be empty before it can be filled," she said, and then shrugged as if to say this much was common knowledge. Standing, she then took up the pot and began to pour more tea into her glass. I was on the verge of telling her that this would be cold also, that I would have Masha warm it, when the tea reached the rim and began flowing over into the saucer. She continued to pour, looking on with delight as the saucer also filled and then spilled over onto the table and onto the floor. She watched until nothing more came from the spout.

"Of course, with God's love"—she set the empty pot back on the table—"there is no end to it. It keeps pouring and pouring."

She seemed to be waiting on me to agree, and so I did, though my mind was still fixed on my carpet and the wasted tea.

She went to the door. "I am needed."

"What do you mean?" I asked.

"I am needed," she said again, and she left. By the time I had gathered my wits to follow her outside, she was already gone from sight, and though I combed the nearby streets, she had disappeared entirely.

I RETURNED THE NEXT MORNING to St. Matthias parish. Asking shopkeepers and various persons in the street, I learnt that the woman I described was a well-known personage in the neighborhood, but her name was not Xenia. She answered to Andrei Feodorovich.

She was, they said, a holy fool, and they proved this by citing miracles she had performed: not only had she predicted the death of the late Empress but there were also boils and rotted teeth healed, a baby cured of grave illness only by her rocking it in her arms. A young woman, it was said, had been prevented from marrying a charlatan by Xenia's warning her mother against the handsome young man. Xenia helped another young woman to marry by sending her to a graveyard where a man was mourning his late wife.

Mostly, these stories were hearsay, excepting one merchant who told me that his own reputation had been saved from ruin by her intervention. Just a year before, he said, in Apostles' Week, Andrei Feodorovich had burst into his shop as he was dipping honey from a barrel for a customer.

"She rushed in and threw herself against that barrel until it tipped. A new barrel, just delivered that morning, and the purest honey to be had. Ask who you will, I am known by everyone to be an honest businessman." He was intent on securing this point before he continued his story.

"Well, all that fine and costly honey spilt across my floor. But then, out from the bottom of the barrel floated a rat. A huge rat! Drowned and bloated and slick as an otter. She saved my good name."

Being a pious man, he had taken a handful of coins from his apron and tried to press them into Xenia's hands, but she let them fall through her fingers. This had left no doubt in him that she was holy.

I asked him where I might find her.

Whenever she came onto his street, he said, he endeavored to draw her into his shop that she might bless the barrels. "She has a taste for honey, and I give her all she will eat." But where she went afterwards, he could not say.

Though everyone seemed to know of her, no one could tell me where she lived. Nor could any say with certainty how long ago she had arrived there or from where, though there was no want of conjecture on this. Some said she had come from a monastery and that she had studied with an elder there to learn their ascetic ways. Others said she had come from some place in the north. When I said that I was her cousin, that I lived across the river and sought her that I might take her home again, they bowed to my claim but with visible reluctance. They seemed to feel she belonged to them.

Wherever I went, she had been there only recently but was not there now. Or someone had heard report of her at another place. Piecing together various sightings, I made my way north and towards the far edge of the parish, which was worse even than the heart of it. Here, every person in the street had such an air of menace that I no longer dared ask after Xenia.

I turned into another street and another, and then she was there, not fifty feet away, walking in my direction and singing some tune. Trailing behind her was a gang of rough boys. They were throwing mud at her. Burbling her private singsong, she tried to disregard their persecution, but when a hard clot hit her in the back of the head it jolted her from her music. She turned and railed at them, thrashing her stick, and chased them back up the street like a fury. I ran after her, shouting her name, and caught her by the arm.

"Xenia," I cried.

She was rocking back and forth on her heels. Her countenance was a study of grief and her lips made fast little burbling noises, a pattern of guttural utterances that were not quite language.

"Andrei Feodorovich?"

My voice did not reach her nor did she respond to my touch on her arm.

After a time, the rhythm of her babbling slowed and began to separate into words.

*. . . to help me Lord make speed to save me Lord make haste to help me Lord make speed to . . .*

Over and over, for I do not know how long a space of time, these same words tumbled like a fast brook, broken only by her breath. Gradually, the words became too soft to hear and only her lips continued to move. Her rocking slowed and at last she grew calm.

"Xenia?"

Her gaze rested on the air. "Listen," she said.

I heard nothing out of the usual. "What? What is it?" I asked.

She did not answer, but closed her eyes. I closed my eyes as well and heard the angry squabbling of a cock, and at a farther distance the faint clattering of wheels and hooves on cobblestone. Perhaps I had misunderstood. I opened my eyes again. Xenia remained just as she had been, a pleasant smile on her lips, like a person lost in reverie.

My poor Xenia. Had she wandered here in these terrible streets all these years, too addled to find her way home? Had something happened to her to cause her to forget herself, to forget where she lived? She had not seemed to know the house when she saw it, or Masha either. She had not called me by name. Perhaps we were strangers in her eyes.

"Xenia?" My voice seemed loud as shattering glass. "We cannot stay here in the street. Let us search out a droshky, shall we?"

She consented to return to the house, and when we had arrived there, I tried to impress on her that this was her home. She need not ever go back to that place. We cleaned the mud from her and washed it from her garments. Masha roasted a duck for our dinner, and she ate it with relish.

When she had eaten, she stood.

"You may have your old bed," I said. "I have put fresh linens on it." I reminded her of the night when she had bequeathed this same bed to me, but if she recalled this, she did not show it. Just as she had done on the previous day, she said that she was needed, and behaved like one who has an appointment to which she dare not arrive late.

I grasped her hand and urged her to sit again. "You are needed *here. Please.*"

"I have a place to be." She said it with good humor but was resolute and would not sit.

I knew not what else to do. I let go her hand. "What place is that?"

"Oh, you know, with God."

"With God. And where is He?" I pressed. If she would go again, at least I should know where to find her.

Assuming a frantic disposition, she mimicked pulling something apart in her hands. "Where is it? Where is the onion's heart?" she wailed in mock despair. "Nothing but onion, onion, onion." She chuckled and invited me to share her merriment.

When I could not, her eyes softened with compassion. "It is all good. All of it. Listen."

And then she turned and was gone.

AGAIN AND AGAIN, I RETRIEVED her from the streets of St. Matthias parish. I found her huddled beneath the eaves of the church, or in some lonely alley or stable, out of the wind perhaps but without even the sheepskin and stockings and boots I had bought for her. Even when the snows came, she remained out in the open. That she did not catch her death is, I suppose, all the proof one might want that she was indeed blessed by God, but it frightened me to see that her feet were black and swollen.

"You think them ugly?" She sat next to me in the droshky, wiggling her toes as though she were delighted by them.

"It's not so much their appearance, but I fear you shall lose them to frostbite."

She shook her head. "They are hard as a dog's pads. Feel." She lifted up a foot that I might touch it. When I hesitated, she barked and made growling noises, then laughed at her jest.

"God lives in my feet. They do not feel the cold."

Not feeling the cold is the mark of frostbite, but I knew there was nothing to be gained by this argument. I might offer her yet another pair of shoes, but if she agreed to take them they would only end up on someone else's feet. By slow measures, I allowed that my love would not keep her here, and I could not be her jailer. Instead, I brought food and clothing to her wherever I found her, until I saw that she did not need this help either. I had this small consolation: for one who lived in the streets and on the charity of her fellow man, Xenia did not want for anything if only she would have it. She would not accept alms unless perchance the coin was stamped with the image of Saint George on horseback—and taking this she promptly gave it away again—but because she was thought to be holy, wherever she stopped on her irregular rounds she was tempted with food. She might walk into a merchant's shop and with impunity help herself to a pickle from the barrel or a fistful of raisins. If she deigned to eat, the merchant believed he would have good luck for the remainder of the day. Similarly, drivers vied to offer her rides so that they might get wealthy customers afterwards.

At irregular intervals separated by a day or a month, she began to call here of her own will. Just as she used to when she still answered to Xenia, she often brought with her a beggar or unfortunate to be fed or otherwise tended to.

It was never only to visit; always she came with some pretext that she was needed. One afternoon, she arrived by coach and burst through the door like the fire brigade, shouting, "Tell Masha to put on the kettle! I am here!" just as though I had urgently sent for her.

I had not, of course, but as it happened, her visit aligned with my feeling my loneliness acutely. I had that morning passed the shop on Galernaya Street where I had used to buy Gaspari's tea. I had turned and gone inside. The merchant, a man in his middle years, was brown and thin as a tea leaf himself. I imagined him to be of Mongol blood, a cousin perhaps of one of the traders who led the camel caravans up from Peking on the tea road. It was said to be a journey of more than a year through mountainous terrain, and breathing in the aromas of the shop I could not help but call up exotic scenes of men dressed in rough furs and turbans and huddled round a smoking campfire, their beasts laden with the precious cargo.

He remembered me, though it had been a very long time, and asked after the health of my husband. I cannot say why, but I did not want to tell him that Gaspari had died, and so I bought a small packet of tea. For the length of my walk home, I had reproached myself for such foolishness. You are as wasteful as Leonid Vladimirovich, I thought, but you do not have a daughter or son who will take you in when you become a pauper. I had made myself miserable with worry and self-loathing.

Now, I offered Xenia the more comfortable chair, but she preferred to stand at the stove. She held her gnarled hands close over the tiles to thaw them. Masha brought the tea, and the room filled with a cottony quiet.

Ours was an odd kind of visiting. She could not be engaged by idle gossip, for what happened yesterday or the previous week did not hold her interest. I had learnt not to ask after her health and she did not ask after mine; the body and its various aches and failings did not concern her. Living so entirely in the present moment had also made her immune to either expectation or worry for the future, so there could be no talk of civic affairs. If I told her of what I was reading, her attention drifted and she would begin to hum.

Indeed, she had so entirely lost the art of conversing that we sat for the better part of an hour without a word passing between us. Strange as it may seem, though, I was not bothered by this. A wonderful peacefulness came to me merely by my being in her presence.

"Do you remember Leonid Vladimirovich Berevsky and his daughter?" I said at last. "Do you remember the evening you rescued her little dog from dancing?"

She gave no sign to indicate whether she did or did not but only sat in that way of hers, smiling benignly.

The steam from my glass unfurled the scents of smoke and camel's sweat. I looked at her and she at me, and in that moment it did not matter whether she recalled any of our shared past or what we had been to one another; in her gaze, I felt utterly and inescapably beheld.

CHAPTER FIFTEEN

I had passed six years as a widow when Kuzma Zakharovich died. Perhaps it was only to observe the forms
that caused Nadya to send me the notice, or perhaps the
years had softened her bitterness towards me. I went to the
house the next morning.

There was a wreath on the door and many persons already in the anteroom. I supposed several of them to be
Kuzma Zakharovich's children. I looked about for my aunt
but did not spy her, nor anyone else I knew. But Nadya was
there with the priest and several others, in the next room
where her husband lay. In the threshold, I watched her
leaning on the arm of a young officer of perhaps eighteen
or twenty years. She was weeping. Though she had always
had a capacity to act what was needed, her grief looked
genuine. It emboldened me. I went to her and offered my
condolences. She seemed faintly puzzled to see me but was
courteous and introduced me to her son, who was a child
when I had last seen him.

"And the baby, little Sasha, is he here also?"

She pointed him out, and two others who had come after him. I confess, I felt a prick of envy, but I was glad for her, too, that she had children to cushion her grief. I admired them to her, and she accepted my compliments.

I asked Nadya if her sister knew of Kuzma Zakharovich's death.

Nadya's mouth hardened. "To what address should I have sent the notice? And to what name?" She did not wait on an answer. "It does not matter. Surely she knew of his death even before I did. Is this not her reputation?"

I agreed that it was.

Xenia was known widely to have predicted the death of our beloved Empress Elizabeth and again, more recently, the murder of the Empress's predecessor, Ivan Antonovich. Poor Ivan. While but an infant, he had been unseated from the throne by Elizabeth Petrovna and then locked away in a dungeon for twenty years. It was said by some that his confinement had deprived him of his wits. And then to be murdered in his cell by his guards, the only companions he had known all his days. On the heels of this sad rumor had come the further rumor that Xenia had predicted it. On the day before his death, it was said, she had walked the streets of her parish, weeping loudly and shrieking of blood.

I was reminded of her dreams. Of her husband's death and the blood pooling round his head. Of her subsequent horror at the sight of her own blood. But the general populace could not know these things. They did not know Xenia, only the holy fool called Andrei Feodorovich.

•    •    •

I LEFT NADYA'S HOUSE AND walked. I altered my route home that I might pass by the old Winter Palace, which was then being dismantled. It was open to the sky, the roof and walls stripped down to the timbers, and birds swooped in and out of what had been the grand ballroom and the reception rooms and private quarters.

The old opera house attached to one end of the palace was still intact; it was being saved for some other use. As I watched, laborers emerged from the open back wall, carting rubbish to the street—heaps of old rope, moldering canvas, and a ceramic shell I recognized, one of several that had once hid the footlights. I followed a laborer inside.

The interior was dim and musty and sadly decayed. Emptied of its chairs and draperies and gilded fixtures, it was like a great beast being stripped to the bone. A few warped backdrops and set pieces leaned against the side walls, and one of these was familiar to me. Most of the paint had flaked from it, but the scene still ghosted from the canvas: stands of palms and hanging flowers, a plashing fountain, faded peacocks and tigers and, like bookends with their trunks raised, a pair of elephants. It was the garden of Poro, the Indian King.

The memory of Gaspari's ethereal voice slipped between my ears, sharp as a newly honed knife.

As I stood in the empty theatre, I remembered that I had now been widowed in almost equal measure to the time I had been married. I was not quite thirty-six years of age, and years stretched before me, years that I would have need to endure without him or children who might remind me of him.

I recalled Xenia saying that this emptiness was sweet. Perhaps the saints are right in thinking that the depth of one's love is measured by the capacity for suffering, yet one cannot help but question those who court it with such fervor. Even Christ, who submitted willingly to his suffering, first prayed that the cup might be taken from him.

THE NEXT WEEK, AS I was sitting at my mending, I heard the sound of Xenia's stick upon the stair. I was glad it was she, for my bleakness on the day of Kuzma Zakharovich's funeral had not left me. I was taken aback, then, when she crossed the threshold shouting.

"Get up!" she scolded. "Why do you sit and sew buttons when your son waits on you?"

"I am Dasha," I reminded her. "I do not have a son. Here." I set aside my mending and patted the cushion beside me. "Calm yourself. I will tell Masha to make us tea."

But she would not sit. "There has been an accident. Your son," she insisted, shaking her head in violent little jerks. "Your son."

I wondered if she had confused my door with someone else's. I knew she visited others; stories trailed her erratic rounds, and among these were accounts of her coming to a house with tidings of death or illness. I could not entirely discount the possibility that somewhere in Petersburg was a woman looking for her son, and Xenia had brought terrible news of him to the wrong address.

"Hurry," she commanded, and she turned and went back down the stairs. There was never any arguing against her. I followed.

She had kept a droshky waiting at the door, and the driver conveyed us over to the Petersburgskaya Storona and then to the particular corner where she directed. A carriage was stopped in the middle of the street, and a crowd had gathered round it. Seeing us alight from the droshky, someone recognized Xenia and escorted us into the crush.

At its center, a young woman lay on the ground, moaning. She had been struck by the carriage. Though it was forbidden to go at a gallop within the city, it was a law widely flouted, and these carriages were a menace. The onlookers said she had been knocked down as it flew wide round the corner, and she was trampled beneath the wheels. There was much blood, and one of the woman's arms lay at an unnatural angle.

However, it was not only from her injuries that she suffered. The woman was large with a child, and the blow had jarred it in her womb. They had tried already to carry her from the street, but the woman was too broken to endure being moved. It seemed evident she would die. Because no one knew her, the woman's family could not be located, but a midwife had been found to do what she could.

I think some in the crowd hoped that Xenia might save her, for they parted to allow us to come next to the woman, and even the midwife did not object when Xenia squatted down and, rocking on her heels, began to whisper soft noises near the woman's ear.

The midwife had made a tent of the woman's skirts and said to me, "Hold up your cloak. At the least, she should not be exposed to all these eyes." I did as I was told. It was a small mercy, perhaps, that the woman was too far gone to take notice of those about her. She lay there with her eyes closed, insensible in her pain, by all appearances near death. Then all at once, her face contorted and she arched up and let loose a long, terrible scream, as though she were being torn apart on the rack. The midwife bid her to bear down, though the woman seemed incapable of hearing. When her pains subsided, she panted jaggedly. Xenia's soft babbling increased.

This continued for what might have been an hour, the woman reviving only when the child stirred within her and caused her to shriek. Increasingly, she was too exhausted even for this and only opened and closed her mouth like a fish. The police came and went away again. The carriage and its occupants left also. Much of the crowd had dispersed and because my arms were too weary, I had long since let the cloak drop.

The woman arched in a final agony, then deflated and went still. "Get the knife from my pack." The midwife reached back a hand without looking and waggled her fingers. She took it from me. "And the rags as well." She reached under the woman's skirts and working there at last extracted a small, bloody mass. She slapped it till a shrill cry broke loose. Then she wiped it clean with the rags and wrapped the scrawny thing in a swath of muslin. She handed me the bundle, no larger or heavier than a loaf of bread, while she finished tending to the poor woman.

Framed in the swaddling was a tiny face, dark and shriveled. Its pale eyes squinted into the light—they were surprisingly patient and knowing. It is perhaps foolish to say it, but I felt I glimpsed some recognition in them— not of me, but of unseen things—as though it had carried into this world some perception from its former realm. I looked to Xenia, but she had gone, slipped away without my notice.

Its mother had died. There being no one to claim the infant, I said I would take it until the family could be found. The weary midwife said it was probably too small to live.

"Poor little motherless thing." She sighed. "It's probably just as well it returns to God."

It was already too late for me to share this view.

For the safety of his soul, I had him baptized at once. I hired a wet nurse, and then we waited to see if he would last the night. He did, and the next day as well, and my anxiety for him lessened by fractions as each day passed. A notice appeared in the *Gazette* of the accident, the death of the woman, and of the surviving infant. I anticipated the grieving husband or grandmother who would arrive at my door. I imagined, too, how their sorrow might be a little lessened when I put this child in their arms. But despite my noble intentions, I was vastly relieved when many weeks had gone by without such a scene. For a year or two after, though, I carried in my breast an apprehension that was awakened by every knock on my door.

I did not name him straightaway, for I did not yet believe he was mine to name. Having need to call him something, I called him Matvey, gift of God. I thought of the son whom God gave to Sarah in her old age. Sarah laughed at God's messenger when he said she would bear a son. She was ninety-nine years old, who would believe such a thing? And who would believe that the widow of a eunuch might also become a mother? But when the child is delivered and put into your arms, how can you continue to scoff?

I will grant it is possible that Xenia may have come upon the carriage accident quite by happenstance. I have considered this myself. She may have perceived that the mother would die from her injuries and then come to fetch me there. Even my poor intellect can conceive an argument against divine interference. But any mother must surely feel as I did when she first holds her child. Against this wondrous and inexplicable goodness, reason is a poor adversary. Matvey was my faith, and I was foolish for him.

When he was older and had need of a patronymic, I gave him Gaspari's name. I did not deceive him concerning his parentage; of course, he knows we are not his true parents. Still, I think of him as our child, as much ours as if he were from our flesh. I sometimes see Gaspari's gentleness in him. I see, also, Gaspari's heightened consciousness of his place outside the tightly drawn circles of society. Without relations to advance his cause, an orphan may breach them, if at all, only by great talents or extraordinary charms. Matvey lacks these—he is like me in this—but he will work at a thing until his back is bent and his fingers raw, and for this reason he has recently found a good position on an estate to the south of Moscow. Though he would not have left

Petersburg otherwise, and though he asked me to move there with him, there was no question in the end but that he would go and I would not. We are like two stout Tatar horses: made for the humble work of pulling whatever is yoked to us. This is our way.

## CHAPTER SIXTEEN

We had only just sat down at table last month when the bell was ringing downstairs. Briefly, absurdly, my heart rose, thinking it was Xenia come to bid Matvey farewell, but she had not visited here for nearly half a year and she never rings. Masha came to the table to say there was a woman downstairs wanting food for her child. "Well, invite her in," I said, but Masha replied that I should come to the door. I excused myself from my company and made my way down the stairs, feeling vexed by each of the fourteen steps to the bottom, and lifted the latch.

The woman on the far side of the door had the thin and exhausted look of one who has lived from hand to mouth for some time. I told her she was welcome and stepped back to let her pass.

"God bless," she answered, but she showed reluctance to cross the threshold. "It's not for me that I come." She drew forward a child hidden in her skirts. Of perhaps three or four years, it was pale and bruised-looking. "I was told I might leave her here. Only for an hour or two."

"There is enough for you as well."

"God bless," she repeated. "It's only that . . ." Her glance strayed nervously to the street. My eyes followed, but there was only the drowse of midday and nothing out of the ordinary. The sky outside had turned woolly, signaling that it would snow before long. I had felt it in my joints since I woke that morning, age making me as prescient as Xenia, though my predictions are confined to the weather.

"I left a blanket," she said. "Near the Anichkov Bridge. I'm afraid someone may steal it. If you will take her, I'll go back and fetch it."

I nodded, and she began to pry the child's fingers loose from her skirt. "The good *babushka* here will look after you," she said. The child eyed me with the wariness of a feral cat and desperately tried to reattach herself to her mother. "It cannot be helped," the mother said sternly, but she was visibly distressed also, and turned and ran away.

I took one of the child's arms. It was thin as dry tinder. "Come," I coaxed. "There is food upstairs."

The others looked up when I returned with a child.

"Where is the mother?" Matvey asked.

"She will be back shortly." I said this to reassure the child, but in truth I did not believe it.

"Here, you may sit with us," I said to the child. Osip slid down the bench to make room next to himself, which was generous, as he has come here almost daily for years now and is very proprietary about his place at the table.

Masha fetched a plate, spooned some cabbage and a bit of sausage onto it, and we resumed the talk the child's arrival had interrupted. Matvey was telling the company what he knew of his new employer.

Although the child was clearly starved, she was too upset to eat. She looked warily round the table, and I cannot say as I blamed her. We made for a strange lot. Besides Osip and Matvey, there was Varenka, who was once a dancer kept by Peter Sheremetyev in his harem until she lost too many teeth and was put out. And next to her, Marie de l'Église, who is stranded here by the troubles in France. There were also Nikita, a laborer Xenia sent here after his leg was shattered in a fall from a roof, and Stepanov-Nelidov. He was formerly a prosperous fur trader, though you would not guess it now. He astonishes me by finding his way here when he is otherwise too drunk to remember even his own name. He eats a little dinner, sleeps, and then takes his leave when he is sober again, full of repentance and devastated courtesy. I am never lacking for company if I do not mind whose company it is.

I have said to Masha that I will ruin myself, just as old Leonid Vladimirovich did, by keeping an open house and table. The jest only half conceals a real anxiety. Every year, I draw water from a little closer to the bottom of the well, and I have feared outliving my money. I also worry that by spending on strangers, I am depriving Matvey of an inheritance. He has never spoken a word of reproach. Still, when I am gone and have left nothing behind, might he not think that I loved him no more than the flotsam that washed onto my doorstep?

In spite of this, I have continued to take them in, those

that Xenia sends as well as those who seem to arrive of their own volition. After Gaspari died, I sent half of his money to his mother, thinking that what remained would be sufficient to keep me. Naturally, I had not accounted for the feeding of so many guests. In spite of every frugality, most of the remaining sum was run through in eight years. To make ends meet, I rented the downstairs of the house, but even this did not cover my expenses. I began to look on each person who came here as another debit and to consider how I might prevent Xenia from bringing more.

Then my father died. My mother, who had been by all accounts in the most perfect health, followed him into the hereafter within a few short weeks. I would not have thought her so attached but have learnt it is unwise to judge these bonds by their outward appearance.

In short, being the only remaining heir, I was left the estate unencumbered, and it was sold. Between the modest proceeds and what I receive in rent from the glovemaker downstairs, I have the means to continue on here for perhaps another two or three years. After that, we shall see. I have no gift to foretell the future, not even from one day into the next.

Seeing that the child would not touch her plate, I excused myself and took her away from the table to a quieter corner of the room. I pulled her onto my lap and rocked her. I hummed aimlessly, following with one ear the conversation that continued at the table. Because Matvey would be stopping one night in Moscow, Varenka was telling him something of the city, though it seems doubtful she was ever there. Without teeth, her speech is very mumbled, but the others listened politely—even Marie, who understands no more than a few words of Russian. All except Stepanov-Nelidov. He has most certainly visited Moscow but could add nothing to the general wisdom, as he had drifted into sleep, his chin on his chest and a light snore emanating from his open mouth.

The child squirmed, then gradually her restlessness slowed, and at last she could not fight sleep any longer. As she drifted off, limp and open-mouthed, her breath was a rasping whisper. I adjusted the sharp little elbow that was digging into my side. Except that her belly distended unnaturally, she seemed not to have enough flesh on her to anchor her to this life. Then again, children are sturdier than I credit them or none would live past his first year. With sufficient bread and meat, who knows.

By ones and twos, my guests excused themselves and took their leave. I do not think a one of them has a particular place to go, but they are careful to pretend that they do. In the worst of winter, some will return here at night to sleep, but even then only the sick remain past the morning.

It was nearly two o'clock when the bell rang again. Two policemen were at the door. The more senior of the two asked for "the one who is called Andrei Feodorovich." I could not tell whether his phrasing denoted honor or suspicion.

"Andrei Feodorovich has been dead now for more than thirty years," I said.

"We are looking for the fool who goes by that name."

I was able to say with honesty that I had not seen her since late spring and, for the moment, to be grateful of this.

"What is it you want with her?" I asked.

"There is talk that this person has spoken out against Her Imperial Majesty and means harm to her." He then cited a rumor that Xenia had been seen in the streets ranting about rivers of blood.

"Yes, yes, so they say." The rumor had been repeated for some twenty-five years, ever since the murder of Ivan Antonovich. "Even if there were anything to it," I said, "it is cold gossip indeed."

He was not pleased by my impertinence. They had been ordered to find Xenia and bring her in.

I expect the recent insurrection in France has made Her Imperial Majesty newly fearful for her crown and alert to any stirrings in the population here. Emigrés fleeing from Paris to Petersburg are bringing with them alarming reports of soldiers and priests and commoners rising up in arms against their nobles and their king.

For all that Catherine is well-loved, it has not been forgotten by some that she came to the throne by means of a coup and that perhaps others had a more rightful claim to it. And while it is strange to think of our most reason-loving Empress being made uneasy by a fool, she would hardly be the first. Elizabeth before her kept poor babbling Ivan Antonovich a prisoner of the crown all her days. Even so, they say, it was fear of him that kept her awake nights. And before that, Saint Basil is said to have caused Tsar Ivan Grozny to tremble when the holy fool presented him with a slab of raw meat, saying that a murderer needn't bother with keeping the fast. Our Sovereign may not herself credit the rantings of fools, but others do, and when the world has gone topsy-turvy, even a fool may be dangerous to the crown. Especially one such as Xenia, who will not keep silent.

"Do you know her whereabouts?" the officer asked.

"She is a wanderer," I said, "and comes and goes according to her own dictates. She may stay for five hours or five minutes, but where she goes after is anyone's guess."

This was not the whole truth. I did not know where she was at that moment, but only recently one of the unfortunates who come here had brought with him a report that she sleeps in the Smolenskoye cemetery. Then again, gossip needs no carriage, and her fame has grown so great that she is rumored to be everywhere, within the city and without it. If all claims were believed, she would be pilgrimming continually from one holy site to another, for reports of her have returned from as far away as Siberia.

"Truly," I added, "there is no cause to seek her further. Andrei Feodorovich would do no harm to anyone. She has been touched by God"—I tapped my temple—"but she always loved Her Imperial Majesty most particularly."

He crossed himself, but instantly put on again his opaque manner and informed me that I was obliged to alert officials if she should come to this house or if I should hear anything pertinent to her whereabouts, and with that they left. I feared for Xenia if the police succeeded in finding her, for she would certainly be unable to give her interrogators satisfaction.

It is a peasant belief that, as we are all equal in God's eyes, He must surely confer on fools unseen, compensatory gifts. And so our peasants attend fools with great reverence and scrutinize their gibbering for veiled wisdom and prophecy. Even the more enlightened prefer them in their charity over the ordinary poor. For this reason, the streets are thick with counterfeit fools who don chains and profit by feigning madness. The credulous lump all these together and call them the blessed ones.

Because I have known Xenia as she was—bequeathed every worldly advantage of wit, modesty, and riches—I know she is not a pretender. At the same time, it is hard for me to accept the loss of these advantages as a sign of God's favor. I should still choose for her the easier blessings.

## CHAPTER SEVENTEEN

As so often happens in Petersburg at this time of year, the sun made its first, brief appearance that day even as it was setting. Unexpectedly, it peeked from beneath sodden clouds, flared, and then dropped into a narrow band of sky on the horizon gone suddenly bright. The world, gray since dawn, saturated with color. On the church, the unpainted brick glowed warm as a stove and the tiny icicles on its cornices glittered. The hem of the clouds was streaked vermilion, and even the air itself was amber as honey. For a few moments everything was luminous, like a hand-tinted drawing. And then it was over. The band of light dissolved, and the sky began to fade.

A new church is being built on the grounds of the cemetery. I have watched it go up for two years, until now only the belfry remains to be finished. This last is the slow labor of ants, for the workers must climb to the top of the scaffold and then pulley up each load of bricks. Recently, though, the tower has grown more rapidly, so that it will certainly be completed soon. The workers know me—I go there most every week to tend the graves—and they will wave when I pass. At that hour, though, only two remained, packing their tools, and they expressed surprise to see me.

"This is no time to visit the dead, Matushka."

I said that I was looking for the fool Andrei Feodoro-vich.

They know of her, of course, but had not seen her about. When I told them that I had heard she slept there, a look passed between the two, but then the larger one shook his head. You should go home, he told me. It will be dark be-fore long.

The driver did not like the idea of my staying, either. I was only able to quell his misgivings by paying him double the usual fare and promising the same again if he would wait.

I set off down the path that cuts to the river, calling her name. My voice carried so loudly in that silent place that she would surely hear me if she was there, though this did not mean she would answer.

In summer, it is a pleasant place to visit. Past the edge of the city, it is so thick with birch and oak that it stays cool even in the worst of the heat. At Easter or in fine weather, there are others about, and I will sometimes see peasants bathing at the river. But now, in the autumn gloaming, the cemetery was desolate. With the floods, every depression had become a pond, and I had need to pick my way with care, stick in one hand, and to leave the path when it sub-merged. I should have been uneasy, alone there at dusk and surrounded by the dead, but I was not. Each marker was familiar: the wooden crosses of the earliest residents, the granite slabs with their more recent dates, the white marble tombs of the well-born.

At last I came to Andrei Feodorovich Petrov's grave, an iron cross and a low fence frosted with new snow. It was deserted, the snow undisturbed. If she had been here, there was no sign of it but only the withered flowers I had left some weeks before.

"Andrei Feodorovich," I called out, for she will not answer to Xenia. I listened for some answering sound. "Andrei Feodorovich, are you here?" If some person were to have come upon me, what might he have thought of my standing at Andrei's grave and shouting his name? But I had no concern of being judged: the place was so empty at that hour that no one would come there who was not himself a little mad.

"It is Dasha. Please. I must see you." This had been all of my plan—to go to Smolenskoye cemetery and find her. I wanted to warn her of the police, though I knew she would not care.

The cemetery was silent as no other place can be. There was perhaps a quarter hour of light left. I should do as I have been advised, I thought, and return home. Instead, I left Andrei's resting place and followed the path to the river. This river separates the Orthodox buried on the left bank from the foreigners and infidels interred on the right. Across the little bridge, the cemetery is new and untamed, the few markers scattered amongst the trees. In death, as in life, they are lonely in their difference there.

His stone is granite, engraved in both Russian and Italian. It was crusted with snow, and I brushed this away. *Francesco Gaspari. 1718–1762.* I brushed again. *Beloved.* The fig I planted in May had dropped its leaves; the first hard freeze would kill it. Every winter, I pull up the dead shrub, buy a fruit, and start another from seed, nursing the tender shoot indoors until it can be planted in late spring. When Matvey was a child, it gave him pleasure to grow this fig for his father, and it became a tradition with us.

I go to Gaspari's grave nearly every week, and as I weed the plot and scrub lichen from the stone I will talk to him. Our conversation is now the reverse of what it once was, with my carrying the weight of it and his listening. I also look to his neighbors that need tending to, those dead, Germans mostly, without family here. After my work is done, I stay on. Though I am not so entertaining as he was, I have found I have much to say.

I tugged on the fig, but it would not pull up. "I'm sorry I did not come last week. Matveyushka came home with news. He has found a position.

"Princess Dashkova—do you remember her? She was a friend to Grand Duchess Catherine, and after you were gone she had a hand in putting her on the throne. Since then, well, you can imagine, her influence has only grown." I used my stick to loosen the dirt around the roots. "Well, our Matveyushka will be overseeing the building of a greenhouse for her and will manage the orchards. He says she has two hectares given to stone fruits—plums and cherries and I cannot recall what else—but most of this is sent to market. She would like a greenhouse so she may have melons and cucumbers when there is snow on the ground."

I yanked again, and continued to work. "He was flush with pride when he told me. For his sake, I made to celebrate. I had Masha bring out a bottle of your Madeira that I had been saving against I know not what. But he will be leaving Petersburg, dearest. And Troitskoye is at best a week from here. It is hard that he will be so far away."

At last, the fig came up. I smoothed over the soil I'd disturbed.

"He wishes me to close up the house and follow him. 'You are too old to stay on alone, Maman,' he said. But how can I abandon the unfortunates? With winter there will be more of them coming to the door."

The offices of love are obscure to me. I have often felt exhausted by this endless procession of the needful—the starving and lonely widows, the old men undone by illness or drink—but it grieved me to think of the door being shut against them. I thought of Martha: Martha who fretted and served and then was rebuked by Christ because it was her sister, Mary, who was doing what was needful, which was only to adore. I pictured these two sisters, and it was Xenia that I saw sitting at Christ's feet and gazing up at him, her face radiant with joy.

"All week, I have tried to think what Xenia would have me do. After all, it is her house, too. But even could I ask her, she would express no view on the matter beyond telling me to listen. She says this and then is no more forthcoming than you, my dear husband. I think she means I should pray, but I have done this. God, too, is silent."

The sky had grown dark, but the snow gave off a little light, making Gaspari's stone and the nearest trees visible. There was a moon.

"I had thought I might find her here. The police came to our door this afternoon. They were looking for her. They said she had spoken out against the Empress. You and I know that cannot be true, but there is such madness afoot in the world these days. All this wild talk of blood and anarchy in France.

"Oh, and there is also a child come to the house today. Her mother brought her and then left. I do not think she is coming back. What then? If I take her to the foundling home, it is little different from killing her outright. I suppose I might take her with me if I leave. But I cannot take them all."

I plucked up the few gray weeds that stuck through the snow until his plot was as clean as a new blanket.

"If I go, there will be no one left to tend to this. Perhaps you should not mind it so much, but I hate the idea of leaving you alone here. If you were in Italy, there would be family to visit you. I am so sorry, *cuoricino mio*. It pained me to leave Petersburg when I thought I would never see it again, but I might have been more cheerful for your sake. There is no use for these regrets. Still, you should know. I would gratefully follow you anywhere now.

"It is so simple to see what I might have done in the past, but I am no wiser for it. No, every year that passes, I know even less. What do you think, is this why I have lived so long? That I should eventually become a fool?"

I am not yet so muddled that I expected an answer, but I stopped talking. I was weary of my own fretting. The moon had risen, so bright that the snow gleamed like silver. I was stiff with cold.

"If I leave, I will come back, *cuoricino mio*." It may be a long time yet, but I have asked Matvey to bury me there, though it is unconsecrated ground.

I kissed Gaspari's stone on the letters of his name. The tenderness I felt for him was so acute that I was certain his spirit was beside me. The dead are not gone, not entirely, not ever.

I returned by the way I came, using my stick, like a blind woman, to feel the lay of the path where it was in shadow. As I approached the cemetery's entrance, the church came partially into view through the trees. By design, all elements of a church—its soaring height and gilded domes and the sumptuous ornament of its interior—are meant to suggest the magnificent presence in the world of Almighty God the Father. However, this church is still unfinished. The belfry is open to the sky on two sides, and the steeple that will top it must be imagined entirely. At night, unpainted and with scaffolding pinioned to the face, it had the insubstantial appearance of an abandoned relic or even a chimera conjured by the moonlight. It was the Holy Ghost that was invoked there, the unknowable mystery.

When I arrived, I had left the droshky at the front, but I did not see it now. It may be that the driver had given me up and left. I was so far from home that if I had to walk, it would take me till morning.

My eyes were drawn again to the face of the church by some movement. I stopped and strained to pull shapes from the darkness, but then decided it was nothing. Perhaps a bird that had made its nest there. Or clouds moving across the moon and playing tricks on the mind. A cemetery at night summons up unreasoning fears.

But no, the shadow was moving. It was not my imagination: a black silhouette was climbing the scaffolding, moving very slowly and steadily up towards the stunted tower. It appeared to be a hunchback. I watched, transfixed. At long last, it reached the top and emerged onto the moonlit platform, and I saw that it was not a hunchback after all, but a thin figure bent under the weight of something carried on its back. It set down this bundle and opened it. Bricks. The apparition was stacking bricks onto a large pile that already awaited the mason's trowel. I did not remember noticing these when I arrived. Having added its bricks to the pile, it then did something even more strange. It bowed low to each of the four corners of the earth in turn. Having performed this priestly rite, it descended again and, upon reaching the ground, disappeared into the darkness. After some moments, it appeared again, hefting another load on its back.

I cannot say how long I stood watching the repetition of this. Or how long before I understood what I was witness to. No sudden spark of perception but, rather, a slow-growing recognition that it was Xenia.

She was climbing again. Once onto the platform, she unloaded her bricks, no more than eight or ten, for this was all she could carry. I might have gone and fetched more to help her, but I did not. Nor did I think to interrupt her work. The need I had felt so urgently to speak to her had left me.

The quiet gathered. It was very deep, this silence, as though the woods and the church were sunk beneath water. I allowed myself to rest into it, to let the silence close over me. My mind also became still and soft. It was like being on the floor of a sea, like being in the drowned city of Kitezh.

Again, she bowed low to the east and held there. In the bleached and shadowed moonlight, her bent figure was like stone. Then she prayed to the west and again to each direction. I imagined the prayers floating up, not only hers but innumerable others, a city of prayers. The air was filled with them. I imagined the waters rising above our waists and then our shoulders and heads. And how I would see this but not panic. I imagined descending into a perfect quiet and letting go all my fears.

I bowed to Xenia, though she did not see me. I thought to myself how she is accustomed to excusing herself when she leaves by saying she is needed. This, I have come to think, is what it means to be blessed.

Upon rising, I wrapped my headscarf more securely and knotted it beneath my chin, feeling grateful for my good boots and for the sturdy feel of my stick against my palm. The moon lit the way out from the cemetery. There was nothing to do but follow the path, to put one foot in front of the other until I reached home.

ACKNOWLEDGMENTS

For all the talk about writing being a solitary endeavor, I was hardly lonely while writing this novel. I had a lot of help.

For assistance in my research, I am indebted to Professor Sara Dickinson, Università degli Studi di Genova; Sister Ioanna of St. Innocent Religious Community in Minnesota; Professor Derek Offord, University of Bristol; and Professor Christine Worobec, Northern Illinois University. For the gift of their perceptive early reads, I am grateful to Lynne Barrett, Debra McLane, and especially to my dear friend Kyra Petrovskaya Wayne for her help with all things Russian. What errors and infelicities remain are mine alone.

I am beholden to Claire Wachtel, a truth teller, for insisting that it must be better and then waiting another year while it got that way; and to Elizabeth Perrella, Heather Drucker, and the rest of the folks at HarperCollins who have turned a bunch of bytes into an *objet d'art* and then sent it out into the world. My thanks to Marly Rusoff and

Michael Radulesçu for their friendship and wise counsel; I am just so lucky to know such mensches. That goes for Rachelle and Mitchell Kaplan; Kimberly and Les Standiford; Ellen Kanner and Benjamin Bohlmann; Michael and Paula Gillespie; and James W. Hall and the Lady Evelyn: our lives here in Miami would be a bust without them.

Everything I write is read first by my husband and in-house editor, Clifford Paul Fetters, and then improved immeasurably by his insights. There are not words enough to thank him for his patience and his commitment to what we do.

And lastly, in loving remembrance of my dear spaniel, Leo, a wise and holy fool in his own way. The muse lying under my desk during the writing of this book, he died peacefully the night before I sent out the completed manuscript.

Insights,
Interviews
& More...

\*

# Meet Debra Dean

© Susan J. Horgan

DEBRA DEAN was born and raised
in Seattle. The daughter of a builder
and a homemaker and artist, she
was a bookworm but never imagined
becoming a writer. "Growing up, I read
Louisa May Alcott and Laura Ingalls
Wilder, Jane Austen and the Brontës,"
she said. "Until I left college, I rarely read
anyone who hadn't been dead for at least
fifty years, so I had no model for writing
books as something that people still did.
I think subconsciously I figured you
needed three names or at the very least
a British accent."

At Whitman College, Dean double-majored in English and drama: "If you can imagine anyone being this naïve, I figured if the acting thing didn't work out, I'd have the English major to fall back on." After college, she moved to New York and spent two years at the Neighborhood Playhouse, a professional actors' training program. She worked in New York and regional theater for nearly a decade, and met her future husband when they were cast as brother and sister in A. R. Gurney's play *The Dining Room*. "If I'd had a more successful career as an actor, I'd probably still be doing it because I loved acting," she said. "I understudied in a couple of long-running plays, so I was able to keep my union health insurance, but the business is pretty dreadful. When I started thinking about getting out, I had no idea what else I might do. What I eventually came up with was writing, which in many ways was a comically ill-advised choice, given that the pitfalls of writing as a career are nearly identical to acting. One key difference, though, is that you don't have to be hired before you can write. Another big advantage is that you don't need a facelift or even new clothes to be presentable: most days, I can get away with wearing my ratty old jeans and T-shirts."

In 1990, Dean moved back to the Northwest and got her MFA at the University of Oregon. She started teaching writing and publishing her short stories in literary journals. *The Madonnas of Leningrad*, her first novel, was published in 2006. It won numerous awards, was a national ▶

> " What I eventually came up with was writing, which in many ways was a comically ill-advised choice, given that the pitfalls of writing as a career are nearly identical to acting. "

**Meet Debra Dean** *(continued)*

bestseller, and was published in twenty languages.

"In retrospect," she said, "I'm very grateful for my circuitous journey, that I wasn't some wunderkind. I like to think that I have more compassion now and a perspective that I didn't have when I was younger." ∽

" I'm very grateful for my circuitous journey, that I wasn't some wunderkind. "

# On the Trail of a Holy Fool

**Debra Dean**

WHILE RESEARCHING for my first novel,
I took a detour and came upon the story
of an eighteenth-century Russian saint.
Although fragmentary, the story went
like this: a member of the minor
nobility, Xenia was widowed at the
age of twenty-six, when her husband
died suddenly. She went mad with grief
and began to give away all her worldly
possessions. Her family tried to stop her
by having her declared insane, but the
judge disagreed. At this point in the
story, there is a gap of seven or eight
years. She just disappeared. When she
surfaced again, on the streets of the
worst slum in St. Petersburg, she was
dressed in the rags of her dead husband's
military uniform and would answer
only to his name. It was rumored that
she slept in the Smolensk cemetery.
She became known as a healer and a
clairvoyant. Famously, she foretold the
murder of the supposed mad heir to the
Romanov throne, and later, the death
of the woman who had imprisoned him,
the Empress Elizaveta Petrovna.

Although fascinated, I approached
Xenia with a Presbyterian reserve. I was
raised in a denomination that values
restraint, self-possession, and committee
work—saints are just so over the top.
Like superheroes, they don't seem
entirely real. And yet . . . Xenia went
mad with grief. There was something ▶

so elemental and human in this. In *The Year of Magical Thinking*, Joan Didion wrote eloquently about the radical dislocation that followed her husband's unexpected death. To love deeply is to risk being undone.

So was Xenia touched by divinity, or merely touched? I recently met a woman who told me that in her training as a psychotherapist, one of her teachers offered up this thought experiment: if Joan of Arc presented herself to you as a patient, how would you treat her? It is a wonderfully Russian kind of question, allowing as it does that judgments of madness and sanity might have metaphysical or social implications rather than being wholly biological.

If Xenia were to show up where I live, I think the chances are very good she would be put on meds. Lots of meds. And if statistics are any indicator, she might well also stop taking them and end up back on the streets again. We've all probably seen her or one of her sisters pushing a wire cart full of soda cans and talking to herself. Crazy? The answer seems pretty evident to a passerby. But sanity is a way of talking about norms, and how we regard those who fall outside those norms says a lot about our society.

These concepts, "normal" and "mad," didn't even exist in Russia until they were imported from the West during the reign of Catherine the Great. In ancient Russia, people like Xenia occupied a place of honor akin to the shaman of Native American cultures. They were

> " To love deeply is to risk being undone. "

strange, but in their strangeness they had access to extraordinary powers and wisdom. When Christianity arrived, these same people were called "blessed" by God. The thinking was that as we are all equal in God's eyes, those with visible deficits must also have compensatory hidden gifts. Consequently, even the babbling of ordinary fools was parsed for veiled wisdom and prophecy. The tsars kept fools on hand in the courts, not only for entertainment but also for counsel. The pious offered them alms and hospitality. Sure, they wandered out in the weather wearing only rags and bells (or in the case of St. Basil, nothing at all), but their position in society was such that the poor sometimes *pretended* to madness as a means to get by. In the Age of Reason, the increasing throngs of crazies and crazy wannabees in St. Petersburg became such an embarrassment that they were deemed a public nuisance. Catherine the Great attempted to solve the problem by simply outlawing begging and almsgiving entirely.

Because how could you know for sure who was deserving? (To put this question in a contemporary light, think of the cardboard signs that read "Will Work for Food" and "Hungry Children at Home.") The question was further complicated by the Russian Orthodox Church, which explained that some of these seeming madpersons—the *yurodivi*, or holy fools—were in truth ascetics who had given up all their ▶

> " In ancient Russia, people like Xenia occupied a place of honor akin to the shaman of Native American cultures. They were strange, but in their strangeness they had access to extraordinary powers and wisdom. "

worldly possessions and then gone one step further: in order to more fully experience the humility of Christ, they had also voluntarily renounced worldly reason and chosen to act like fools.

That got me. As much as I love some of my things, I can imagine giving them up. But to relinquish my powers of reasoning? My intellect is my stock-in-trade as well as a personal vanity, and I have spent all my life trying to do the smart thing or, at the very least, avoid looking stupid. When, unavoidably, I act like an idiot, I just hope like hell no one is watching. It's not that I can't imagine losing my mind, but to part willingly with it—and worse, to choose that humiliation without even the anesthetic of genuine idiocy—is no casual act of piety; it is stepping into the abyss.

Writers are like dogs burying and digging up the same bones, over and over again. In *The Madonnas of Leningrad*, I had grappled with this question of how much or little we need to survive, of what is truly essential. My protagonist's journey through Alzheimer's was also an exploration of who we might be, absent our intellect, and what of value may lie on the far side of reason. I wrote to the end of the book without arriving at answers. There was still the scent of meat on that bone, so I dug it up again.

There are a couple of different ways to read the story of Xenia. One is that she went mad with grief—an involuntary response worthy of our pity—and in the throes of this mental illness she gave away all her possessions, moved onto the streets, and suffered pointlessly. Or—the way the Orthodox would have read it—she knowingly rejected her culture's attachment to material possessions and rationality in favor of a different wisdom. This radical peeling-away left her open to receive gifts denied others: the ability to heal and forsee the future—in short, the ability to perform miracles.

Initially, I gravitate to the first version. After all, I live in a culture that adheres to the belief that there is such a thing as "normal." Those who deviate from that set point—and the American Psychiatric Association is continually expanding its list of disorders—those people should be treated. Ours is also a culture that believes (even against its own statistical evidence) that more is better. So what clearer definition of insanity could there be than to deliberately divest oneself of all possessions and choose a life of penury?

Yet I cannot stop there. When we sift every experience and idea through the strainer of rational thought, we risk discarding what is strange but amazing, what is precious and true: art, love, beauty. Reason is the blunt instrument the sciences have used since the time of Catherine the Great to bludgeon the arts and religion and leave them for dead. But it is a false dichotomy. Lately, the front edge of science is starting to look pretty crazy, too. When astrophysicists ▶

> " When we sift every experience and idea through the strainer of rational thought, we risk discarding what is strange but amazing, what is precious and true: art, love, beauty. "

**On the Trail of a Holy Fool** *(continued)*

propose with straight faces a universe in which one could time travel or see the back of one's own head, it gets harder to dismiss the miracles of saints as just so much childish superstition. "There are more things in heaven and earth, Horatio, than are dreamt of in your philosophy."

Or to repeat Woody Allen's joke at the end of *Annie Hall*: "This guy goes to a psychiatrist and says, 'Doc, uh, my brother's crazy, he thinks he's a chicken,' and the doctor says, 'Well why don't you turn him in?' And the guy says, 'I would, but I need the eggs.'" ∽

# Have You Read?
## More by Debra Dean

### THE MADONNAS OF LENINGRAD

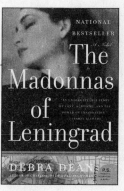

Bit by bit, the ravages of age are eroding Marina's grip on the everyday. An elderly Russian woman now living in America, she cannot hold on to fresh memories—the details of her grown children's lives, the approaching wedding of her grandchild—yet her distant past is miraculously preserved in her mind's eye.

Vivid images of her youth in war-torn Leningrad arise unbidden, carrying her back to the terrible fall of 1941, when she was a tour guide at the Hermitage Museum and the German army's approach signaled the beginning of what would be a long, torturous siege on the city. As the people braved starvation, bitter cold, and a relentless German onslaught, Marina joined other staff members in removing the museum's priceless masterpieces for safekeeping, leaving the frames hanging empty on the walls to symbolize the artworks' eventual return. As the Luftwaffe's bombs pounded the proud, stricken city, Marina built a personal Hermitage in her mind—a refuge that would stay buried deep within her, until she needed it once more.

**Have You Read?** *(continued)*

"Dean writes with passion and
compelling drama." —*People*

"Rare is the novel that creates that
blissful forgot-you-were-reading
experience. This sort of transcendence
is rarer still when the novel in question
is an author's debut, but that is precisely
what Debra Dean has achieved with her
image-rich book."
—*Seattle Post-Intelligencer*

A surprised Southern matriarch is confronted by her family at an intervention. . . . A life-altering break-in triggers insomniac introspection in a desperate actor. . . . Streetwise New York City neighbors let down their guard for a naïve puppeteer and must suffer the consequences. . . .

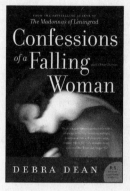

In this stunning collection of short stories, bestselling, award-winning author Debra Dean explores the modern experience of life lived with one eye on the audience. "Her characters are actors, the ones who get paid and ones who are acting out or acting happy or acting brave." (*Miami Herald*) Dean's *Confessions of a Falling Woman* is a haunting, satisfying, and unforgettable reading experience.

"Smart . . . gritty and real . . . Debra Dean's new collection is proof that the [short-story] form can capture gripping, neurotic, or darkly funny slices of life in a way that illuminates the modern experience on a broader level."
—*Chicago Tribune*

"Readers will certainly forget themselves in these sparkling stories, pausing over small, strange moments that change entire lives."       —*Publishers Weekly*

Don't miss the next book by your favorite author. Sign up now for AuthorTracker by visiting www.AuthorTracker.com.